A Candlelight Ecstasy Romance ™

"I'VE BEEN WAITING FOR YOU TO GROW UP, JESSIE."

Trying to catch her breath, she whispered nervously, "I am now."

The moment she had fantasized about for years was here. His hands moved slowly down her sides, exploring the ripe outline of her hips. Then, ever so slowly, they began to slip under her T-shirt and glide up her bare back, the touch of his fingers searing her tender flesh with each new caress. A raging fire was unleashed in her, and Jessica felt herself being drawn closer and closer by some dangerous and delirious force, responding in a way she had never dreamed possible.

LOVE, YESTERDAY AND FOREVER

Elise Randolph

A CANDLELIGHT ECSTASY ROMANCE™

Published by
Dell Publishing Co., Inc.
1 Dag Hammarskjold Plaza
New York, New York 10017

Dell ® TM 681510, Dell Publishing Co., Inc.

Candlelight Ecstasy Romance™ is a trademark of
Dell Publishing Co., Inc., New York, New York.

ISBN: 0-440-14715-8

Printed in the United States of America
First printing—June 1982

Dear Reader:

In response to your continued enthusiasm for Candlelight Ecstasy Romances™, we are increasing the number of new titles from four to six per month.

We are delighted to present sensuous novels set in America, depicting modern American men and women as they confront the provocative problems of modern relationships.

Throughout the history of the Candlelight line, Dell has tried to maintain a high standard of excellence, to give you the finest in reading enjoyment. That is now and will remain our most ardent ambition.

Anne Gisonny
Editor
Candlelight Romances

To Jim, for his persistence,
his encouragement,
and above all his belief in me

CHAPTER ONE

The air was charged with a feeling of expectancy, provoking in Jessica an oppressive sense of dread. The cold, relentless wind, bone-piercing in its intensity, wrapped itself around her and penetrated the seams of her expensive woolen overcoat, forcing her to hunch her shoulders and hug the coat more tightly to her body.

The city was bracing itself for the celebrations of St. Patrick's Day. The signs of it were everywhere. Decorations hung from traffic lights. Paper leprechauns, stuck haphazardly on office windows, peered lifelessly at passing pedestrians. Even the Chicago River, normally gray and uninteresting, flowed green and impatient with the added volume of dye. The two-week-old snow, into its second stage of thawing and refreezing, congealed to the bottoms of Jessica's boots as she walked south on Michigan Avenue.

"So what are you going to do to celebrate tomorrow

night?" Bill inquired, raising the collar of his coat to cover his neck.

"Oh, not much of anything," Jessica replied to the man she was walking with, her mood dismal at best. "I'm afraid I don't much go in for this sort of thing. Besides, I have some accounts I need to work on at home."

Holidays depressed Jessica. She disliked celebrations of any kind, especially raucous ones like St. Patty's Day, which seemed such a frivolous waste of time. Nothing more than drunken revelry, ostentatious parades that tied up traffic, and green—green everywhere! Even more importantly, holidays always awakened the painful memories she wanted to forget. No, she had no room in her structured life for holidays.

But then, it had not always been so. There was a time, as a child, when she would have loved nothing more than to perch atop her father's shoulders and watch the mayor and the floats and the crowds with a sense of childish wonder and delight. Then every holiday was a major event in her life, and every event a holiday, filled with excitement and love, anticipation and fulfillment.

She pushed aside the disturbing thoughts and quickened her steps as if she could physically move away from the memories, leaving them to dissolve in the snow behind.

Bill leaned toward her. "You really shouldn't work so hard, you know. Everybody needs some time off just to play." He attempted to smile, but his frozen facial muscles refused to budge. He continued speaking through lips that barely moved. "I'm going to be meeting some friends at the Brassary after work tomorrow night and from there, who knows where we'll end up? Why don't you join us? It's got to be more fun than sitting home alone and work-

8

ing, and . . . well, I'd really like it if you would come." His eyebrows were raised slightly in anticipation of her answer. Jessica started to say no; the independent loner, ready with her stock answer. But then, maybe it would be nice to be with Bill and his friends, and Heaven knew, it had been so long since she had been out on a date.

Bill Jenkins was a certified public accountant for one of the biggest accounting firms in Chicago, and was hoping for a partnership by the end of the year. In fact, he had interviewed Jessica and offered her a job when she was first trying to decide on her own employment. He was only thirty-three and his meteoric rise in the firm attested to his ability and drive. Jessica couldn't help but admire his meticulously groomed looks as well.

She had never accepted any of his invitations for dates before. Though he had tried repeatedly to engage her in more than an occasional lunch, she had remained cool and aloof, preferring to retain the business relationship they had thus far established.

But if there were to be someone special in her life, if she ever decided to fill that particular void, a man like Bill Jenkins would be ideal. He was kind and considerate— always the perfect gentleman. And most important of all, he did not seem interested in her background or her wealth; it was her intelligence and expertise in finance that he seemed to respect. She knew, beyond a shadow of a doubt, that he thought of her as an equal, and at this stage in her life she wouldn't even consider a relationship with a man who did not.

Studying his polished, Ivy League appearance and distinctive good looks, Jessica concluded that a relationship with Bill would, most likely, be very pleasant. Safe and equal and consistent.

Tomorrow night probably would be fun. Her other, Spartan self would not hold her back this time. She would go and she would have a good time. Despite the cold in her cheeks her own smile began to widen. "Okay, Bill. I'd love to go."

"Great!" He was obviously happy. "I'll meet you at the Brassary by six o'clock."

"Fine." They had turned onto Randolph Drive and were entering the Standard Oil Building.

Jessica liked the looks of this building, the fourth tallest in the world. It's lines were clean and vertical, uncluttered by decorative appointments; a representation of the way she wanted her own life to be. Quietly simple and unencumbered by superfluous relationships.

Bill seemed to know almost everyone in the restaurant, called Stanley's, and stopped with a brief hello at several different tables. They settled on a table by the window overlooking the courtyard and fountain. Here they could watch the Batavia wind chimes. Hundreds of thin copper strips, set close together in a vertical pattern, extended ten to fifteen feet in the air. As the copper shafts swayed against each other in the wind, their contact produced a delicate melody. Though the chimes could not be heard inside, the swaying motion had a reassuring and calming effect on Jessica.

"I brought those SEC brochures for you." She dug into her briefcase, her hand claiming the packet of information from the Securities and Exchange Commission that she had promised to bring him.

As Bill tore open the envelope containing the pamphlets, the waitress took their order.

"Did you want the quiche today, Jessica?"

"That's fine."

10

"Okay, two quiches." He held two fingers in the air and smiled at the waitress. After she jotted down their order and left, Bill turned his attention back to the pamphlets. "Listen, thanks for bringing this info." He had spread all the booklets out on the table.

"You're welcome." Jessica leaned across to point at a particular brochure. "That one has some really good tips on generating cash flow and increasing the yield of your stock portfolio."

"Sounds like my kind of investment," Bill said, laughing.

"Hey, Jenkins!" Their conversation was interrupted by another friend who had just walked to their table and grasped Bill's shoulder. Unaware of Jessica's startled intake of breath, Bill responded to the man.

"Stephen! I didn't know you were in town. God, it's been ages! How have you been?"

"Great," was the dry response, but the man's eyes told a different tale. They were shadowed by a look that was tense and brooding.

"I'll just bet you are," Bill smirked. "I keep up with all your escapades through the gossip columns, you know. Who is it this time?" he leered jokingly. "A fiery redhead neatly tucked away in a medieval castle in Ireland? No? A luscious brunette on the French Riviera?"

While Bill kidded him about his love life, Jessica appraised the familiar face of the man standing before her. He was as devastatingly handsome as she had remembered, with the same strangely compelling combination of honey-colored hair and dark brown eyes. He was tall, well over six feet, with a lean, athletic build, and his skin was bronzed by perpetual sunshine—a glowing contradiction to the bloodless gray winter of Chicago. His angular features were chiseled into an expression of immovable arro-gance, but the insolence was tempered somewhat by an unfamiliar strained look, a look that harbored the scars of some private emotional battle.

The figure of the man before her was an older, more hardened Stephen, and she was shocked by the cold, malevolent look in his eyes.

Stephen did not answer Bill, but instead stared directly at Jessica, his discontented eyes boring into her face, a slight inquisitive frown forming between the brows. The light from the window gave his eyes a reddish cast as they roamed her face with penetrating thoroughness. His gaze lightened almost imperceptibly as he took in the familiar gray-green eyes and the delicate, soft features, but glazed over with hardness at the sight of the dark brown hair pulled severely off her shoulders and clasped high in the back, accentuating the defiant tilt of her chin, her mouth held thin and tight and slightly anxious. As his eyes low-ered they fixed on the shape of her breasts rising nervously now under her silk blouse.

Although only his eyes had moved across the planes of her face and chest, she had the strange sensation that he had touched her—invaded and conquered her somehow—and she felt an electric jolt shoot upward from the base of her spine.

With a traitorous loss of breath Jessica averted her eyes from his face, but the image of it remained imprinted in her mind. Bill introduced them, but there was no need to do so; she knew who he was.

"Hey, I'm sorry, Jessica. This is a friend of mine, Ste-phen Dalheurst. Stephen, this is Jessica Benchley. She's my stockbroker and my—friend," he added quickly.

"Jessica." Stephen's voice seemed to claim her name, as

his possessively questioning eyes drilled into her every feature. She felt the heat blazing from them, although she avoided eye contact with him. Finally she lifted her eyes to meet his.

"Hello, Stephen. It's been a long . . ." She turned her face from him, unable to complete the sentence. He said nothing, but the frown on his face deepened.

"You two know each other?" Bill inquired, looking from one friend to the other.

Jessica merely nodded. She didn't trust herself to speak. She knew who and what Stephen Dalheurst was, and she was disgusted with her agitated response to his presence. *Go away, Stephen!*

Sitting stiff and awkward in her chair, avoiding the stares of the two men, she felt the years tumble away, leaving the unwelcome memories exposed and raw before her.

She was nineteen, and the day was like copper: all shiny and burnished with reds and golds. Everything seemed so much more intense in autumn, the world so much more alive in its last fiery breath before winter.

Benchcrest stood stately and dignified, the purity of its whiteness enlivened by the vibrant colors of nature surrounding it. The terraced lawn sloped gently downward from the house more than a hundred yards to the rocky cliff that dropped sharply to the lake below.

This far north of the city, Lake Michigan was beautiful. It was clean and unfettered and somewhat capricious. Jessica liked to watch the sky-hued water lapping at the rocks below, sometimes in gentle caresses and other times with violent surging slaps that shot foam halfway up the side of the cliff.

As a young child, she had been warned time and time again to keep clear of the edge. But time and time again she was drawn to it as if by a magnetic force, a force that compelled her to defy her parents' order. She loved to sit on the tip of the rocks, imagining it to be the edge of the world, with the lake representing the vast eternal space beyond. She would let her feet and legs dangle precariously in the air while the breeze brushed recklessly against her face and neck and arms. In her childish innocence she felt endowed with an unearthly sense of power. She would stay this way for hours, it seemed, until her brother or mother found her and scolded her all the way home, making her promise that she would not go there again. She always promised, but she was always drawn back to her perilous spot.

But now she was a young woman, and her parents no longer worried about her falling into the lake. She was finally free to sit there and indulge her mind with dreams.

"Isn't your mother worried you'll fall off the cliff, little girl?" Jessica had been gazing out over the lake, absorbed in her private thoughts, and did not hear footsteps approaching. She turned quickly and saw Stephen Dalheurst looming above her, his feet spread wide apart and his hands on the sides of his waist. In the sunlight his hair shimmered with a tawny glow; his eyes were the color of mahogany. It had been a long time since she had seen him. He had been living in Europe for the last year on a large sailboat, so elaborate that it could only be called a yacht. Immersed in the opulent and lavish world of the ultrarich, he was known to be equally at ease in the company of rock stars or royalty. How much older and more worldly he seemed to Jessica. And still so fiercely handsome.

"And isn't your mother worried about when you're

going to grow up and get a job, little boy?" Jessica retorted, her cheeks flaming at the mere sight of him. Little did he know that she had been sitting there building a fantasy of the two of them together. Little did he know that, since she was fifteen years old, her every sensual fantasy was of him.

"I had forgotten what a smart-alecky little brat you are." Stephen sat down beside her, letting his legs dangle next to hers.

"First of all, Mr. Big Shot Jet-setter, I'm *smart,* not smart-alecky. And if you had half a brain, like you're supposed to have when you graduate from Harvard, then you'd notice that I'm no longer a little brat. I'm in college now, you know." She stuck her tongue out at him playfully.

Stephen was very quiet for a moment, studying her, his eyes traveling in a slow seductive trail from her head to her toes.

"Well, you're right about the last part anyway. You've turned out much better than I thought you would."

Jessica wasn't sure if his statement was a compliment or not, but she took it as one. Stephen Dalheurst had gained a reputation throughout high school and college as quite a ladies' man. All of the girls Jessica knew had been, and still were, in love with him and he, naturally, had reveled in his own popularity. He had favored a different girl every week, discarding each one as a new pretty face caught his eye. But Jessica knew that he belonged to her. In her mind he had belonged to her for years. And her skin burned with excitement at the physical closeness of him.

She also enjoyed his teasing her. It made her feel older and proudly sophisticated—more on equal footing with him. She couldn't help but goad him a little too. She *was* a smart aleck. She knew it. She had always been too quick with a tart tongue, too ready to criticize and poke fun at others. And, though she nearly always meant it in a humorous fashion, she had lost more than one friend from her too honest wit.

"So . . . what did they do? Kick you out of Europe for breaking too many hearts?" *Please say you're here to see me! Please!* she begged silently.

He laughed. "No, but I'm sure it will happen sooner or later. Why aren't you out chasing college boys like all the other sexually liberated coeds?" he challenged, looking at her with an unfamiliar, seductive glint in his eyes.

"Because"—she affected her most sophisticated look—"there aren't any college boys around worth chasing." *Because I want a man not a boy,* she wanted to add. *I want you.*

Jessica had expected him to retort with another insolent remark, and when, instead, his features shadowed with sudden seriousness, her heart began to flutter in a wild staccato beat.

"Looking at you sitting there like that reminds me of the time—you couldn't have been more than fifteen or sixteen—when that little boyfriend of yours broke your heart. Remember?"

She remembered. But her recollection of the event was probably nothing like his, she thought bitterly. She had fallen in love with Stephen then, a love she had never got over.

"Yes, I remember." Her cheeks began to color, and she turned her face from his. "You always were good at soothing my little aches."

"As I recall, it was not such a little ache to you. You were really hurt when that kid starting dating someone

16

else. Don't deny it." He smiled as he watched her shaking her head. "And I must say"—he directed his look squarely into her eyes, and the pink in her cheeks deepened almost to a bloodred—"I wanted to beat the hell out of that punk for hurting you the way he did."

"No!" she exclaimed, shocked by this admission. Surely he hadn't felt about her the way she felt about him. No, he must have meant that in a brotherly fashion, nothing more. But if only—

"Does that surprise you so?" Stephen asked, but received no response. She was watching him curiously, not daring to believe that he had felt something for her other than fraternal affection.

"Does it shock you to find out that I cared about you?"

"I knew you cared about me," she admitted reluctantly, accepting what she already knew to be his true feelings. "After all . . . you were like a . . . brother to me."

"A brother!" he scoffed. "Is that why you think I was so upset, why it tore my heart out to see those tears running down your cheeks?"

Jessica brushed aside a lock of hair in agitation. What was he saying? This was so frustrating! She had thought of no one but him for so many years, but she never dreamed that he had thought that way about her. And she knew he didn't. Yet, the things he was saying. . . . it was all so confusing, so—

"Didn't you have any idea what you did to me every time you felt compelled to tell me the details of your love life?" He was leaning closer to her now, and she could feel the warm flow of his breath. But she could say nothing. She could only wait and hope that she was not misunderstanding what he was saying. "I nearly went insane listening to you confess about which boys had kissed you and

17

when and where." He laughed grimly. "You were all sweetness and innocence and you had no idea what you were doing to me. . . ."

"You never said anything! You never even hinted that —"

"Said anything? No." His face was contemplative. "You were my best friend's kid sister, and well . . . I must have seemed like an old man to you."

"No!" she denied quickly. "You never seemed too old for me. I—" She was embarrassed to continue.

"Jessica?" The name hung heavily in the air. She leaned toward him slightly, shuddering with an eager, vague expectancy. A long silent moment passed as their eyes locked in the knowledge of what was about to happen. Stephen grasped her shoulders firmly and pulled her body into his, encircling her with his arms. His eyes were smoldering, the warm brown liquid in them scalding her lips as his mouth descended toward them. His mouth took hers hungrily, greedily, claiming her quivering lips with an unexpected but urgent need.

She was nineteen, almost twenty, and she had been kissed lots of times, but never, never the way Stephen was kissing her now. His mouth drew back slowly, his eyes possessive in their gaze.

"I've been waiting for you to grow up, Jessie."

Trying to catch her breath, she whispered nervously, "I am now." The moment she had fantasized about for years was here, and instinctively she knew exactly what to do.

She arched her back slightly and slid her hands up his arms, closing around his neck and pulling his head down to meet her own rising mouth. She sensed a slight reluctance in his desire as his shoulders stiffened, only seconds before a moan escaped his lips and his mouth crushed against hers. His hands moved slowly down her sides, exploring the ripe outline of her hips. Then, ever so slowly, they began to slip under her T-shirt and glide up her bare back, the touch of his fingers searing her tender flesh with each new caress.

A raging fire was unleashed in her inexperienced body, and Jessica felt herself being drawn closer and closer by some dangerous and delirious force inside herself. Her heart was pounding against Stephen's chest, and she felt herself responding in a way she had never dreamed possible.

"You're mine now, Jessie. You'll always be mine." His voice was breathlessly strained. He leaned over her, gently pushing her shoulders backward to the ground. His mouth began to explore the hollow of her throat, and his hand moved to her breast, lifting her bra up in one deft motion. His gently teasing fingers caressed the nipple, hardening it to a stiff peak, his touch sending electrical currents of desire coursing through her veins.

Her own hands were roaming possessively across the broad expanse of his back, tapering down to the slim, jean-clad hips. The storm of sensations raging inside her prompted her to move her hands freely across his body, touching him where she had never touched a man before. It seemed so right with Stephen, so good and natural. He made her feel like a woman, made her experience sensations she had never felt. Her nerves trembled with the awareness of his warm, skilled fingers kneading the flesh of her stomach, then slipping between her skin and her jeans.

"Do you know what I want of you, Jessica?" The hoarse caress of his voice compelled her beyond all bounds of reason or morality. She could only nod in consent to his question.

With one forearm beneath her knees and one under her back, he cradled her body, carrying her into the adjacent woods; the lake, still visible through the trees, bore witness to their intimacy. There, in the gentle warmth of his embrace, Jessica discovered the mysterious and delicious secrets locked inside her body.

After the union of their bodies had satisfied their most intense desires, they lay wrapped in the security of each other's arms. The sounds and smells of the forest were intensified by Jessica's own heightened senses, its autumnal fragrances blending with the heady, provocative scent of two bodies perfumed by the act of love.

Brushing the leaves from her hair and body, Stephen's eyes held a sad, vacant look.

"Did I hurt you, Jessie?" He lifted her fingers from his chest and kissed the tips of each.

Dazed, she shook her head slowly, searching for something other than sadness in his eyes.

"It shouldn't have happened this way. I never intended —"

"Stephen?" Jessica's voice was tentative and weak. What was the matter? Had she done something wrong? "If I've done something . . ." Tears were beginning to well behind her eyes; her voice strangled in her throat.

His hand reached out and cupped her cheek, his thumb tenderly stroking her mouth. "No, Jessie." His voice was as painful as his eyes; his words hung cavernous in the still air around them. "It's just that I shouldn't have—" He paused and sighed heavily. "You are so young. You are *too* young." He turned his head and looked out on the lake, his dark pain directed toward the smoothly undulating water.

"Teach me, Stephen," she implored. "Teach me what you want."

When he exhaled, his breath had a ragged sound. His hand reached out to touch the tender, inviting skin, but it froze in midair, afraid to descend and take what was so freely offered.

"Tell me to get out of here, Jessie. Tell me to go to hell."

"No."

"Jessica."

"Don't go, Stephen. I don't ever want you to go." Her voice was soft and silky, the sound of a woman who has just awakened to her own sexuality and realized all of its powerful, heady sensations.

The air finally loosened its hold on his hand, and it gently fell to rest on her stomach. As he stroked and caressed her abdomen and breasts his eyes followed the movement of his hands, resting on her face for a moment. His voice carried the hint of a sigh. "You are beautiful, did you know that?"

"With you I feel beautiful," she said, smiling, her voice still shaky from the tumultous emotional reactions of her body. "You aren't—aren't going to leave me . . . are you?" Her eyes were pleading with him.

He pulled her up against him, crushing her naked body against his. "No," he said huskily. "I'm not going to leave you."

She could not control the shiver that rippled through her body, a mixture of relief and excitement and cold air attacking her nerves.

"You're cold," he said, responding to her quaking form beneath his. "I'll help you dress."

"Do we have to?" She didn't want to put an end yet to the glorious discoveries Stephen had helped her make.

He hesitated, a look of torment flashing across the surface of his eyes. But his voice, though soft, was decisive. "Yes. . . . We have to."

Pulling her to a sitting position, he slipped her T-shirt over her head, guiding her arms into the sleeves. After slipping her jeans over her feet and ankles, he stood her in front of him and pulled them up over her hips. Kneeling down, he fastened the zipper and snap, then unexpectedly lifted her shirt and kissed the bare skin of her stomach.

In silence she watched him dress, but her hands would not remain idle. She reached out to button his shirt, her forehead resting on the hard wall of his chest.

"I can't walk you to your house, babe." His hands were on her shoulders, his eyes tormenting her with their smoldering glaze. "If your mother saw me . . . well, I'm afraid I'd give us away," he smiled.

She lowered her eyes, staring at the sliver of ground between them, every blade of grass imprinting itself in her mind with intense clarity.

"Hey, don't look so glum. I'll come back this evening."

She looked up at him with excitement. "Tonight? Really?"

"Sure. We'll go out. I'll take you someplace nice, and we'll get to know each other—on a different level."

"Okay." Whatever he wanted, she would do it. Just as long as she could be with him, that was all that mattered.

"Just promise me one thing." His eyes narrowed ominously.

"What?" she asked in apprehension.

"Just promise me you won't mention anything about any of your boyfriends."

"I promise!" she said with emphasis, a laughing gleam in her eyes.

After kissing her softly on the mouth, he turned and made his way through the thick stand of trees between their houses. Jessica watched until he disappeared in the dense woods. She felt numb. Numb and weak and bewildered. The moment of discovery was over. The experience about which she had fantasized had finally unfolded. Though her senses had never been so alive, she heard nothing but the echo of his breath and heart, felt nothing but the fading touch of his hand against her breast and stomach, and the bruising remnant of his lips crushing hers.

It was so long ago, yet she still felt the shame and regret at her foolishly eager response. She would think the pain was behind her, and then suddenly the memories, like sleeping dragons, would rear their ugly heads and glare at her with recriminations.

She had waited hopefully for him to come that night. She had waited, but he never came. Throughout that long, torturous night, she kept telling herself that some unexpected and uncontrollable obstacle had prevented him from coming, that he would have if he could.

It was only the next morning, when she saw the screaming headlines blazoned across the paper, that she realized just how stupid she had been: Stephen Dalheurst had gone to Aruba with a famous model-actress who was filming a motion picture there.

Jessica had loved him, and he had crushed that love. And she would never let another man hurt her the way Stephen had done. Never again!

Her memories were broken by the commanding voice.

Stephen was asking her something, forcing her into the harsh reality of the present.

"What did you say?" Jessica's voice was barely above a whisper.

"Where are you living now?" His tone was disturbingly sharp as he continued to drill through her soul with his eyes.

"Oh . . . I live off Lake Shore Drive, north of Division.

"You're not going to give me your address, is that it?" His voice was full of scorn.

She was uncomfortable with his tone and with this line of questioning. She looked at Bill and he, too, seemed stiff and ill at ease. He could plainly see the effect Stephen's presence was having upon Jessica.

The food arrived at that moment, and Jessica was released from answering Stephen's question. She knew he noticed her relief and he seemed wickedly amused by it. But, she realized, he was not going to let her off that easily.

"Which firm do you work for, Jessie?" He smiled with pretended innocence, fully aware of the effect the old nickname had on her; an effect that grated painfully at the raw edges of her nerves.

She was stunned. No one had ever called her Jessie but her family—and Stephen Dalheurst.

When she mumbled the name of the brokerage firm, her voice was tremulous, a quality that Bill couldn't help but notice. He was about to come to her rescue by changing the subject of conversation when Stephen turned to go.

"I'll be in touch, Jessica. See you later, Bill."

As quickly as when he disappeared from her life seven years ago, he was gone. Jessica sighed heavily with a mixture of relief and defeat. For seven years she had struggled to erase the image of his face, his touch. But here he had just stood, in person, gazing down at her with those handsomely rugged features and smoldering eyes, mocking her long, exhausting efforts to forget him.

"How . . . *well* . . . did you two know each other?" Bill probed. It was obvious that he was straining for an accurate picture of their relationship. He was a little mystified and upset by the encounter, and Jessica knew that the heightened color in her cheeks did not help to mollify his curiosity.

Damn Stephen Dalheurst for doing this to her! The memory of him kept all her wounds open and bleeding. He represented everything she wanted desperately to forget—the isolation of wealth; the shattered dreams; and the distant, fragile life she had been born into.

"He was a friend of my brother's," she managed. "I hardly knew the man."

Jessica sensed Bill's unbelieving eyes riveted on her face as she lifted the shaking fork to her mouth.

"I didn't know you had a brother," Bill said with interest.

"Yes, he . . . was eight years older than I."

"Was? You mean he's—"

"Yes. He was with my parents when they—when their plane crashed." Jessica looked out the window at the chimes, but the image did not reach her mind. She was thinking of what she had once had and lost. She still had the material things, the wealth, the things that did not matter. But she had lost the only things that really held any meaning for her: the security of a family, her passion for life, her need for love. These things were so far back into the dark and hauntingly shadowed tunnel of her past they seemed lost to her forever. Just as Stephen seemed lost to her forever.

"I guess we'd better go now." Bill seemed hesitant to intrude on her memories, but he was right. They both had to get back to work.

As they left the restaurant Jessica leaned on Bill's arm, taking comfort in the solid, undemanding friendship he offered. His presence was just the armor she needed to ward off the cruel army of destructive memories that was besieging and demoralizing her mind.

CHAPTER TWO

She had not slept well last night and could not shake the troublesome feeling that was nagging at her. She couldn't define it other than knowing that, in some way, it had to do with seeing Stephen Dalheurst again. As she walked to work she tried to force the thought away, tried to erase the image of him standing beside her, prodding her wounds with his dark, penetrating eyes.

The buildings of the city rose impressively around her, dwarfing her significance. The Wrigley Building loomed big and white behind her left shoulder, an architectural eccentricity standing shamelessly amidst contemporary high rises. Chicago was like that. Its architectural blends of old and new gave tribute to its spirited past and innovative present. Here was a city that claimed fame to such noted individuals as Al Capone, Saul Bellow, Marshall Field, and Mrs. O'Leary and her cow. Its history was speckled with sensationalism and dramatic events—the Great Chicago Fire, the Columbian Exposition, the St.

Valentine's Day Massacre, and the radical sixties Days of Rage.

Jessica had reflected often on Chicago's colorful past and present and on its heart. She loved its vibrancy, its architecture, and its people. Nevertheless, she longed persistently for the beauty of Benchcrest; for the thickly wooded ravines traversing the estate where she grew up, and for the jagged cliff overlooking the often moody, but always spectacular, lake.

This morning, however, she forced her thoughts away from home, directing her attention to her destination as she turned onto Wacker Drive and headed toward the stock brokerage firm.

She was late getting to work today, a totally unheard-of phenomenon for Jessica, and that fact alone was enough to irritate her. She prided herself on her punctuality and her ability to manage responsibility. And, too, she preferred to arrive at work early so that she could keep on top of the market. The New York Stock Exchange had been open for half an hour already. Opening the office door, she hurried quickly inside to escape the bitter cold.

Here in this office was her raison d'être. This was where she found the only excitement in her existence. Her sense of anticipation was stimulated by watching the Dow Jones averages move up and down the scale. She had clients who benefited from bull markets and other clients who benefited from bear markets, so each fluctuation in stock prices brought challenge and suspense to Jessica. Here was the energy of life: high finance—generating a heat so intense, a force so powerful, it could build and destroy fortunes in a matter of days, or even hours.

Upon entering the office, Jessica rubbed her cheeks vigorously with her gloved hands, returning the circulation

28

to her icy skin. In moments it was flushed with a natural pink glow. She removed her camel-colored coat, navy crocheted tam, and brown calfskin boots. She pulled her tan pumps from her purse and slipped them onto her stocking feet. Smoothing the wool skirt of her suit, she walked to her desk, feeling alive and self-confident, the troubling thoughts of her sleepless night left outside in the cold. Several other brokers were already in the office. It was a competitive business and they, too, wanted the edge.

The morning progressed quickly enough. She had quite a few clients to call, promoting options on an oil stock that was expected to rise dramatically within the next few days. From the firm's New York office they had received an all-out buy recommendation on that particular stock, so Jessica had her work cut out for her.

The nation's economic recovery—when it finally came —was expected to be rapid and explosive, and to bring the stock prices of most of the major corporations up with it. It was a perfect time to have money invested in the market. Even though, for herself, Jessica was too realistic to believe that life offered perfection, it was an agreeable time in her life; steady and without emotional demands. Until yesterday.

At ten thirty the buzzer on her phone pierced the analytical quiet of her thoughts. Before clicking off her computer terminal, Jessica jotted down a figure on a notepad. She answered with a tone of confidence in her voice, listening attentively as the office manager asked her to come into his office. She replaced the phone onto its cradle with the same confidence that she had picked it up. Mr. Caldwell had been pleased with her work there since she was hired four years ago. He had, on several occasions, openly praised her record in sales transactions, holding her up as an example for the other account executives to follow. Wanting to retain her superior standing in his eyes, she walked quickly to his office.

"Morning, Jessica. How about a cup of coffee?"

"Good morning, Mr. Caldwell. No, thank you." She emphasized the refusal for coffee with a shake of her head.

Bob Caldwell was sitting behind his enormous walnut desk, stacks of computer paper and green cardboard files covering every square inch of desk space. The walls of the office were paneled in walnut as well. On one wall was a collage of family photos that Bob had taken. Jessica had complimented him before on his photographic ability, noting the pride he exhibited in showing them. They were good, and he should be proud of them, she thought. They captured vividly the innocence and whimsy of his young children and the serene and rather regal qualities of his wife, Joanne. Jessica had met Joanne Caldwell at a Christmas party a couple of years ago and was immediately struck by the difference between her and her husband. Where she exuded a tranquil beauty, Mr. Caldwell was effervescent and animated.

In each corner of the office were large potted plants. There were areca palms, dracaenas, ligustrums, aralias, and an exquisitely symmetrical Norfolk pine, all furnished and cared for by an interior landscaping company. Once a month someone stopped by to remove any plants that were dropping leaves or turning brown, replacing them with vibrant new ones.

At first Jessica didn't notice the man standing by the window, looking out at the traffic moving spasmodically along Wabash Avenue. But when she saw those square, rugged shoulders and long, lean back and legs, a jolt of alarm shot through her. He turned and confronted her with a boldly amused face.

"Hello again, Jessica." His brown eyes flashed with malicious delight at her lack of composure.

"He-hello, Stephen."

"I understand you two already are friends, so I guess there's no need for introductions." Mr. Caldwell beamed. He looked immensely pleased with the established relationship and appeared eager to move on to the topic of business. Jessica, confused and ill at ease, said nothing. Avoiding Stephen's unflinching stare, she looked intently at Mr. Caldwell to explain the situation.

"Mr. Dalheurst here has asked that you represent his account with our firm." Mr. Caldwell's smile had decreased to the proper size for discussing business matters.

A look of amazement crossed Jessica's face, and she found herself speechless. Receiving no verbal reaction from her, Mr. Caldwell continued.

"I told him, of course, that I was sure you would be delighted." Jessica's expression held no trace of delight, but Mr. Caldwell was either oblivious to that fact or simply chose to ignore it. "Mr. Dalheurst seems more than willing for you to make all decisions concerning his stock purchases." He turned toward Stephen and raised his eyebrows as if reconfirming this statement. "However, he would like, naturally, to be informed of any transactions you plan to make. Now . . . if you two want to work out the specific arrangements for your relationship—your business relationship," he qualified—"then I suggest you use the conference room for privacy."

Jessica's gaping mouth finally began to form words. "I hardly think, Mr. Caldwell, that I'm experienced enough to handle Mr. Dalheurst's account. I—"

"Nonsense. You are one of the best brokers we have. You are perfect for this account." Dismissing the subject and the woman from his mind, Mr. Caldwell waved his hand impatiently, concluding, "I have every confidence in you."

"But an account the size of Mr. Dalheurst's," she argued, feeling a lump of panic rise in her throat, a panic that had nothing to do with lack of confidence in her ability and everything to do with Stephen Dalheurst. Defiance, etched permanently in her character, forbade her to submit passively to Stephen's intrusion into her professional life. Hadn't he done enough damage to her personal life? And why didn't he say something? He just stood there with that sadistic glint in his eyes, as if he enjoyed nothing more than watching her squirm. Finally his voice sliced the tense air.

"Oh . . . *Miss* Benchley"—he emphasized the formal name—"and how do you know the size of my account?" Not only was he openly mocking her but he was making her look like a fool in front of her boss. Her face flushed with embarrassment and anger.

"I don't—I mean, I just assumed. I—"

"Miss Benchley"—Mr. Caldwell's tone stung her with its impatience—"why don't you take Mr. Dalheurst into the conference room—*now*—and there you can get all of the information you need." He was annoyed with her for the first time in four years, and all because of Stephen Dalheurst. His presence was creating havoc, not only with her senses, but also with her job. It was now obvious that she had no choice. She would have to go with him to the conference room. But later—later she would definitely have a talk with Mr. Caldwell. She would simply explain to him that she did not want to handle this account. She had that right. Didn't she? He would understand, she was sure of it. He had to. For the first time in her career, she did not look forward to opening a new account.

Her cheeks inflamed and her blood boiling with anger, Jessica quickly turned on her heels and stormed out of Mr. Caldwell's office. She turned around to see if Stephen was following, but he was still standing there smiling impudently at her.

"Are you coming . . . *Mister* Dalheurst?" She forced the question through clenched teeth.

Jessica led the way into the conference room with Stephen following. His footsteps behind her set her nerves on edge.

The conference room was utilitarian in concept, yet it held the warmly elegant look of financial success. Any client who sat in this room would feel assured that his money was in good hands. Jessica seated herself rather dejectedly in one of the soft brown leather chairs at the round table, and Stephen followed suit.

"Stephen . . . I hardly know what to say." The defiance had left her face; an involuntary awkwardness made her cast her eyes downward. "I really don't think I'm the best person to handle your investments." Jessica was looking at his face now and wondered why she was trembling.

"Oh?" taunted Stephen, a derisive smile playing across his face. "And just who *would* be the person to handle my investments, then?"

"Well . . . I don't know. Perhaps one of the men in the—"

"One of the men?" He laughed mockingly. "And I thought you were one of these liberated types. Yet here you are, trying to turn over one of the biggest accounts I'm sure you've ever had to a *man*. I'm surprised at you,

Jessica." He shook his head, then chuckled softly. "But I must say, I'm relieved. I don't much go for this feminist breed."

"No, I suppose the femme fatale is more your type." Jessica spat out the words at him with tight lips. Stephen didn't reply, but kept his gaze directly on her eyes, penetrating and dissecting her emotions until she was sure that she would drown in those unfathomable chocolate pools.

"Why don't you want my account, Jessie?" A haunting look darted across the surface of his eyes, then darkened to a transluscent and somewhat vacuous stare. She didn't know how to answer him, for she wasn't even sure of the answer herself. Surely what he did to her seven years ago, taking her virginity—and every ounce of her love—and then discarding her as if she had no more substance for him than a used piece of paper, was enough to make her hate him; was enough to make her never want to see him again, much less conduct business with him.

On the other hand she was a professional now. But was she enough of one to put aside her emotions for the sake of business? Yes, she concluded, she was. She had struggled for too many years in a male-dominated profession to destroy all of her gains now because of one man. She was a professional businesswoman and, by God, she would act like one! But her answer sounded tentative. "I do want your account, Stephen. It's just that—" She sighed heavily, knowing there was no way she could tell him her true feelings. She decided to change the subject. "Shall we get started?"

The unconcealed amusement in his expression returned as he watched her busily laying out forms, files, and paper on the table. She was conscious of his penetrating stare; she could feel the warmth of his breath only inches away from her face and wanted nothing more than to run away. An inexplicable fear was building inside her. She could feel it in the prickling of her skin, the perspiration in the palms of her hands, the tingling in her spine. Or was it fear?

"First of all," she said too quickly and too loudly, as if she needed to drown out the traitorous voices inside her, "we need to see how much you want to invest, where you have money invested in the market now, and the type of earnings you would like to receive on your money. The idea, of course, is to seek new and more flexible ways to achieve your investment objectives. For instance"—she did not even stop for a breath—"are you more interested in dividends from safer securities, or are you thinking more about high-yield, short-term stocks? Or are you just wanting to diversify?" She breathed deeply. When he did not answer, she turned her head to look at him and suddenly her voice began to tremble. "I . . . I might—I might suggest a few—"

"It's been such a long time, Jessica." His hand reached out to her shoulder, burning the imprint of his hand into her flesh. His voice was low and husky, and the half-whispered breath of words flowed over Jessica's neck and face, inflaming her cheeks with color. "You've turned into a beautiful woman," he breathed. "But then I always knew you would."

As his hand slid possessively down her arm she felt a familiar but suppressed heat building inside her. Her pulsating blood leaped through her veins, and she felt a quivering ache inside her stomach and limbs. His touch produced a fierce temptation to react as she had once reacted to his touch: hastily and eagerly and completely.

While, on the inside, heat raged through her body, a

35

cold anger surfaced at the involuntary emotion she was experiencing. Her face reflected this anger, and she directed her frustrations at Stephen.

"As I recall, I was nothing more to you than a skinny, smart-alecky brat." Her voice, hiding the bitterness she felt, was sarcastic and her expression haughty. She kept her eyes cast downward so that he would not know the turmoil that was seething within her.

"Oh . . . is that really *all* you recall?" His words were slow and precise, blanketed in velvet smoothness.

His hand moved from her arm to the back of her neck. She was caught in the clasp of his large hand as it guided her head toward him. She was looking at him now; her eyes shone with a mixture of fear and excitement and reproach. She felt his warm breath touch her lips only a second before his mouth crushed them beneath its force.

It was a punishing kiss, but in the dim recesses of her mind she realized that she was responding to his mouth, parting her lips so that his tongue could explore and taste every hollow and corner, her body instinctively leaning toward his, wanting and needing his touch. The taste of his mouth filled her with a delicious sense of urgency.

His hand kneaded the back of her neck, his fingers pulling at her soft brown tendrils of hair. She had not tied her hair back this morning, leaving it instead to fall naturally around her shoulders. Her lips were bruised by the fierceness of his kiss. As his other hand lifted to grasp the mound of her breast, she felt almost powerless to resist him.

But through the restless desire within her body the voices of the past still spoke to her, and the painful memories won control of her conscious mind. The years of empty loneliness had hardened her feelings. Jessica had been forced to create her own form of protection, had learned to listen only to the directions of her mind, ignoring the needs of her heart. She had built a wall around herself, keeping out all of the hurt and cruelty in the world and imprisoning within herself the silent ache of unfulfilled desire; she had built a strong wall—and she would not have it destroyed by Stephen. There was no way she would ever let him know what he had once meant to her. She would never give him the satisfaction of knowing that he had hurt her just as he had probably hurt dozens of other women. Her heart would never be his again to crush.

She thrust herself from him, glaring with a cold stare that masked the fire beneath. "If that is all that I was supposed to recall"—her tone was as precise as his had been—"then it would have been just as effective to remind me verbally. Now, do you mind if we get back to business, Mr. Dalheurst?"

"Well, *Miss* Benchley, you have a slight sadistic streak in you, don't you?" His eyes had turned to brown ice, the look in them hostile and hard as he spoke. "I never would have guessed that." But when he paused, a sardonic smile played around his mouth, and he said, "I wonder . . . when someone reminds you of a simple kiss, do you always react with such, shall we say, fervor?"

Her cheeks burned with embarrassment, the color in them heightening to a deep rose. Why was he doing this to her? The sadistic streak was in him, not her, and she hated him for it. He was turning her insides upside down, playing with her emotions, delighting in her shifts from hot to cold to hot again. Her eyes blazed with this knowledge, and she wanted to scream at him, to flail her arms at his face, to hurt him in the only way she knew how. But before she could strike out at him, he asked calmly, "What was it you were going to suggest I invest in?"

Again she was twirled in the opposite direction, her angry emotions bouncing off the walls of the conference room. It took all the self-control she could muster to regain her cool composure. After a long moment she had collected herself enough to recall what it was that she was going to suggest.

She turned quickly back to the papers on the table, avoiding any further contact with his eyes. But, as she resumed talking of stock purchases, she knew he was watching her. She talked rapidly and wasn't even sure if he was listening to her. He said nothing, but she could feel the heat from his uneven breathing and from those eyes, which seemed to bore into her, as if attempting to unlock the hidden secret door at the bottom of her soul.

After ten minutes of her nonstop talk she saw him stretch and lean back in his chair. "Oh, this is rather tedious, isn't it. I had no idea so much was involved." The statement was uttered very casually, very convincingly, but Jessica was looking at him as if he had lost his mind. Did he take her for that much of a fool? Here was Stephen Dalheurst, who manipulated fortunes—his and others—on a daily basis. Then it suddenly dawned on her: This was all a joke! He had been patronizing her, teasing her, taking her away from real clients—all for a sadistic joke. The revelation stung the backs of her eyes, and she had to fight to keep back the tears of frustration and lost pride.

"Why are you doing this to me?" she muttered, bitterness creeping into her voice.

"Because," he drawled, "I like hearing you talk. . . . I wanted to hear your sales pitch."

"Your money is already fully invested in the market,

isn't it. You had no intention of using me as your broker."
She felt defeated and used, and her voice reflected it.

"Correct on the first statement, incorrect on the second," he informed her complacently. "You must realize that with the amount of money I have, a certain amount of it is already going to be invested in the stock market. Not all of it, of course. I like to keep diversified."

"Of course." Her voice was dry and tight, emotionless and subdued.

"But I *am* transferring my account to you. It's a sizable amount of money, and I will be making lots of trades for which you will represent me. I don't think I have to remind you of the substantial commissions those will mean for you." His look was smug, and she glared at him with open hostility.

"And I don't think I have to remind you that I don't need your money. It's probably tainted anyway. I'm sure that whatever money you have to invest, you no doubt bled from some poor, unsuspecting sucker. So I don't want it."

He chuckled smugly. "Everybody wants money, Jessica, tainted or otherwise. Even spoiled little rich girls like you. Besides," he added before she could interrupt, "the whole idea behind the profession that *you* chose is to make commissions. Remember?"

"I remember." Her chin was high, and her lips were compressed into a thin line of contempt. "What do you want—everlasting gratitude for these crumbs you're tossing me?"

"A simple thank-you would suffice," replied Stephen arrogantly as he stretched his firm torso, pressing his back against the leather chair.

Suddenly the tension, the painful memories, the absurdity of the situation, the foolishness of her ridiculous sales speech, all bubbled into hysteria, and she began laughing uncontrollably. With very little provocation the laughter could have become tears, but with Stephen now laughing, too, the tone of the meeting lightened considerably. When the laughter finally subsided, Jessica was holding her sides from the ache in them.

"Why don't we go to lunch and we can finish up back here this afternoon?" Stephen asked, smiling.

Jessica watched that smile forming, that easygoing smugness return to his face, and something snapped. The levity of a moment earlier vanished, leaving her with a new wariness. She had let down her guard, and the laughter that had been missing for so long from her life had returned. It felt good. It felt good to laugh at the silliness of life—but not with Stephen. She would not lose control with him. If she began to enjoy his company, he would crush her as he had done before. She must remain aloof, not allowing herself the chance to be hurt.

"No," she stated flatly, but with a sound of determination. She had no intention of working on this with him all afternoon. She had other clients too. "Stephen, there really isn't that much to do if it's just a matter of switching your account to me. Why don't you just look over these papers now, and then you can be on your way." At the risk of sounding rude, she added quickly, "I know you have so many other important things to do." The words themselves were pleasant enough, but she was unable to keep the derisive tone out of her voice.

"I'm tired, Jessica. I would like for us to go to lunch now and finish this up afterwards." His tone was no longer pleasant; the lines of his face were set in an immovable expression that suggested he was used to having people do exactly as he wished.

Well, thought Jessica scornfully, *he may be able to control other people's lives, but I'll be damned if he's going to control mine.* "I'm sorry, Stephen," she replied in her most businesslike tone, "but I'm sure Mr. Caldwell would want me to spend some time on my other work today."

The minute she said it, she realized it was a mistake. Stephen jumped up from his chair, a brisk determination to his gait carrying him down the hall to Bob Caldwell's office. Before Jessica could stop him, he was knocking on the door.

"Yes, Mr. Dalheurst. How are things going? Is Jessica taking care of you all right?"

"Yes, Bob," he began, using the familiar name even though Caldwell had not. "She's doing a marvelous job. However, I'm a bit confused and weary over all this high finance stuff and I thought perhaps you would allow Jessica to spend a few hours with me over lunch and then back here at the office to work on this—portfolio, is it?" Jessica was enraged at the deceit in his voice. Pretending he didn't understand high finance, using his most charismatic tone to bend Mr. Caldwell to his will! And she could see by the look on Caldwell's face that Stephen had succeeded. How could a man like Mr. Caldwell be so blind!

"Of course, Stephen. Take all the time you need." Bob Caldwell was putty in Stephen's hands.

Well, thought Jessica icily, she would go to lunch if she had to and she would work with him on his *portfolio* this afternoon. But that would be it. She would tell Mr. Caldwell tomorrow that she was not going to handle Stephen's account. He would simply have to find another broker.

As Stephen turned to Jessica in the hallway, his hand

extended to take hers, she saw the imperious glint of amusement in his eyes, the supercilious arrogance in the crooked tilt of his mouth, and she thought once again how despicable he was.

All right, Stephen Dalheurst, you won this round. But we'll see who wins the next one.

CHAPTER THREE

They were seated in Lawry's, with its round emerald-green booths, the ubiquitous seasonings of the same name on every table. The atmosphere was quiet and peaceful, but the turmoil of her thoughts reflected the opposite. Jessica tried to concentrate on the waitress spinning the restaurant's famous salads on a cart next to the table. But her thoughts kept switching to the man across the table from her.

In appearance he was the same Stephen. That fascinating, uniquely colored hair that looked like fresh-spun honey combined with disarming eyes that were the color of steaming hot chocolate on a cold winter's day. There was a virility about him—in the tanned features of his face and the rugged set of his shoulders—that was compelling. But appearance was where the familiarity ended.

What had happened to the Stephen she had grown up next door to? The Stephen she had known seven years ago? That man had warm, laughing eyes, a carefree though somewhat cavalier disposition, and a gentle, teasing voice. The Stephen before her now appeared to have none of these characteristics. His eyes were cold and hard, clouded by a malevolent dark glare. His voice was sarcastic, carrying none of the laughter that she remembered so well. Watching his expressions as he surveyed the restaurant and its patrons, she felt power emanating from his every gesture. There was something in that hard expression that looked dangerous, and she realized that this man, whom she had known as a brother and a lover, was now a stranger.

She was startled to hear her own mouth voicing her feelings. "What happened to you, Stephen? You are so different." She had not meant to say that, and she blushed at her own audaciousness.

"Time changes people" was the evasive reply. "Besides," he added, "I could say the same thing to you."

"What do you mean?"

"I mean, I'm not the only one who is different." There was a hard edge to his voice, and the brown in his eyes was muted and dull. "What changed you?"

"If I've changed," she retorted, "it's because I have more reason to have changed."

"Oh?" he drawled. "And what is that reason?"

She looked at him in disbelief. The years of agony had been real to her. The pain had colored her every thought and deed. If she had had him to help her over those rough years, maybe things would have been different. Perhaps she would still be the carefree girl she once was. "Maybe you've forgotten that my whole family was killed in a plane crash." There, she had said it. She had never before come right out and stated it that way. It sounded so final and definite. Always before, their deaths had been veiled in vague references, lessening the impact of their tragic, violent end.

"I haven't forgotten," he growled angrily, his eyes thunderous clouds in the golden tan face. "Don't forget Thomas was my best friend."

"Then why didn't you even come to the funeral?" The bitter cry flew from her throat, her face consumed with anguish.

"I couldn't."

"What you mean is, you just didn't give a damn!"

She looked away, unable to believe the scathing remark that had just flown from her mouth. Why had she said such a terrible thing to Stephen? Thomas had been his best friend! She knew he must have been as outraged and dismayed by his death as she was. When she turned to face him, she noticed a dull weariness in his eyes. "I'm . . . sorry. . . . I shouldn't have said that. I—"

"Jessica, no." Stephen reached out to grasp her hand, but she pulled it away from his touch. "I'm the one who is sorry," he continued, his hand resting uselessly on the table. "I never had a chance to tell you." His voice faltered, a buried emotion surfacing briefly to the hardened exterior.

"It was a long time ago," she explained, as if to lessen the grief. It had been a long time. Six years. But she wanted suddenly to talk about it, needed to talk about it after all these years. "It was Thanksgiving."

"Yes," he replied to the known fact.

"Mother and Dad had been in New York with Thomas at some architecture exposition." She laughed bitterly and glanced at Stephen. "He was going to be another Frank Lloyd Wright, you remember."

45

Stephen, knowing it was not expected, did not reply, but his eyes never left her face.

"They were on their way home." Her face was drawn, a bleak tightness to her jaw and mouth. "Dad was an excellent pilot," she cried, choking back the burning but unanswerable questions that had plagued her mind for six years. "The plane was a new Learjet," she added on a more even note.

"They never found out why, did they?" As if sensing that she didn't want his comfort, Stephen held back, not reaching out to take her hand. But his question gave her time to bring the dignity and composure back into her voice.

"No."

The prime ribs came, and they both realized they had not even touched their salads. The conversation had dulled her appetite somewhat, but she began mechanically eating the salad in front of her.

"Why don't you live at Benchcrest?" Stephen's question startled her out of her gloomy reverie.

The troublesome feelings and questions that had surfaced from the conversation about her family had left her weak. She hated this impotent feeling—the feeling her emotions were getting the better of her. She had worked for years at keeping them in check and she didn't like the effect Stephen's presence and his disturbing questions were having upon her.

Jessica never returned home after her family died. She rented an apartment by the university and then, after graduation, bought a town house in the city. With the help of an attorney she made arrangements to keep the estate running. The housekeeper and her husband were to remain there and make sure that everything was the same as always. Jessica paid the bills and had the final say on any major repairs or improvements, but she had not set foot through the gates of Benchcrest for six years.

When she looked directly at Stephen, her face revealed the disdain she felt for his intrusiveness.

The light in the restaurant had subtly changed. Winter-gray, blocking the sun's rays, had spilled a hushed pallor through the windows, leaving everything with a dingy, washed-out appearance. Stephen's eyes dulled to a dark, brooding coffee color when he noticed her haughty expression. She had not answered him, and his next words reflected his impatience. "Well, why don't you at least go there and make sure the place is still in good condition?"

"I really don't think it's anyone's business if I go back or not," she insisted, indignation fueling the blaze in her eyes.

Undaunted by her defensive tone, Stephen argued, "A place as beautiful as Benchcrest needs a master. It should not be left in the hands of servants. It needs life." His voice was scratchy with unexpected emotion. "It needs more than just occupants."

Jessica was shocked by his impassioned remarks. Was there more to Stephen than appeared on the surface? He spoke of her home as if it were his, as if he loved it as much as she did. But no, that couldn't be; it was just another of his ploys to upset her. He was simply trying to twist her emotions inside her and taking sadistic delight in her misery.

Then she raised her head high, tilting her chin up and out, and glared at him with open dislike, a look that stated plainly that she knew what he was up to, that she was on to his tricks. The emotion immediately faded from his eyes, and the cold hard look returned.

"Why don't you just sell the damn place." He turned his head quickly and looked out the window, the expression in his eyes hidden from Jessica. "You'd make a bundle on it."

Jessica suddenly lost her appetite. She pushed the pieces of meat, the Yorkshire pudding, and the sourdough bread around her plate, arranging and rearranging them into new piles. Sell the damn place! God, but he was coldhearted. A couple of months ago her attorney had approached her about selling Benchcrest. He even mentioned that someone was interested in buying it. But she had refused his advice, and she certainly would refuse Stephen's.

A piece of real estate that should be gotten rid of, a way to make a buck. It all came down to that in the end—a stupid lousy buck! What did he understand about memories and love and sorrow? His eyes saw nothing beyond a thing's monetary value. Sell Benchcrest for money?

"I will never sell Benchcrest, Stephen."

Something in his eyes flickered. It was a change in his expression, a change so subtle that she could not interpret its meaning. But it was a definite change. She was sure of that.

Stepping out of the warm shower, Jessica glanced at her watch on the counter. Five o'clock. She still had an hour before she was to meet Bill and his friends at the Brassary. Sighing heavily with fatigue, she rubbed the towel over her body and limbs to warm her skin. She was exhausted from the long emotional day with Stephen. The battle of words and looks had sapped her energy. And yet, she felt a strange exhilaration at the thought of him. Though her mind held a distinct dislike for him, the fluttering in the pit of her stomach was a remnant of the intense physical force that pulled her toward him.

She picked up her emerald-green velour robe from the stool and slipped it on. Taking another towel, she bent at the waist and rubbed her hair dry, then wrapped it turban-style over her head. Using the first towel to wipe the steam from the full-length mirror, she paused at the reflection before her, analyzing the image of herself.

She pulled the towel from her head and let the thick dark brown hair fall to her shoulders. Even wet, the natural waves were there, bending and curving the strands in a soft sensuous shape. Her eyes, a grayish green that seemed to change color with her temperament, held a somewhat lost look now. She had never noticed that insecurity in them before. Had it always been there, or had her intense emotions from the events of the day something to do with it? Her lips were full but not wide, giving a slight bow shape to them. But they were set in a line indicating proud determination and a certain stubbornness. Though a little worried about the diffident look in her eyes, she was nonetheless pleased with the overall image in the mirror.

Did Stephen find her attractive? He had said she was beautiful. Beautiful? She had never considered herself a beauty. Pretty, maybe. But beautiful? She untied the sash of her robe, letting it fall open to her sides. Her body was long and slender, her breasts high and firm, her slim waist curving out to meet the supple line of her hips and long smooth legs. Did he find her desirable? She quickly closed the robe with a shiver. What on earth was she thinking? Was she losing her mind? Why should she care if he thought she was desirable or not? She hated him! She couldn't care less what he thought of her! And yet

. . . she couldn't deny that he awakened sensations in her that she had not felt for so many years.

Just the thought of his hands against her flesh or his face breathlessly close to hers made her heart catapult. She musn't think these things! She mustn't! He had hurt her so badly before. If she weakened to him now, she would never escape his clutches. Why did he have to come back? Her life was finally becoming just what she wanted—unemotional and secure. Why couldn't he just leave her alone? She was leaning her head against the mirror when her eyes caught the reflection of her watch on the counter. Five twenty! Damn! She had wasted so much time thinking about Stephen that now she would have to rush to make it in time to meet Bill at six.

Actually she was looking forward to the evening, and she was more than glad for the diversion. She desperately needed something else—someone else—to occupy her thoughts tonight. She had to get Stephen out of her mind.

The first part of the evening passed pleasantly enough. She arrived at the Brassary, a favorite after-work bar, at six o'clock on the nose. Bill and his friends were already there waiting. As she walked cautiously down the ice-covered steps from North Michigan Avenue, she noticed the bar was already packed with people wanting to get an early start on the celebrations.

Bill was watching the door and came toward her as she entered. He was decked out in a complete western outfit, from cowboy hat to boots, and when she spotted him in the crowd, she had to bite her lip to stifle a giggle. She shouldn't have been so surprised. The cowboy mystique had been filtering into northern cities for several years now. But Bill! She supposed he wanted to present some sort of macho image. But even in his western duds poor Bill still looked like a La Salle Street accountant.

The friends he was with all seemed to be enjoying the celebration, and before long Jessica found herself lost in the fun of it all. The three other men in the group were accountants from Bill's office, and they each had dates. One of the girls was an accountant also, another was a secretary, and the third worked as an account executive for an advertising firm. Jessica couldn't remember when she had had so much fun just enjoying an evening out on the town with friends. Maybe she had shut herself off too much from the rest of the world. But she had found little in the last few years to celebrate about. Still, being with Bill made her realize that she had been missing lots of fun. He was especially comfortable to be with, even if he was playing the urban cowboy to the hilt with his *y'all*'s and *thank ya, ma'am*'s.

He demanded nothing more from her than she was willing to give. They smiled and talked easily, and Jessica felt as if the wounds inflicted throughout the day by Stephen were, if not healed, at least soothed by Bill's presence.

After a few drinks at the Brassary, they gorged themselves on appetizers and French onion soup at the Great Gritzbe's Flying Food Show, then made the rounds of all the bars and discos in the Rush Street area.

"I'm really glad you decided to come tonight, Jessica."

"Me too, Bill." They were on the dance floor, and in his arms Jessica felt relaxed and at ease.

"I hope it won't always take a national celebration for you to go out with me," he laughed. "If so, maybe I'd better go on and ask you out for Memorial Day."

"Well, I guess, like the Mad Hatter, we could always

51

celebrate our unbirthdays." They both laughed and glided across the dance floor. She was having a wonderful time. At a little before midnight all that changed.

They were at She-nannigans, a popular singles bar, where green-vested waiters proclaimed a mood of Irish high spirits all year round. The crowds were beginning to thin somewhat, and the drinks were making her feel all soft and warm and loose inside.

She was casually looking around the bar when she met Stephen's steady gaze, directed at her. Shocked to see him and uncomfortable with his stare, she shuddered and turned quickly back to Bill, hoping Stephen didn't know that she had seen him. What was he doing here? Whom was he with?

After a few minutes, she chanced a glance back at his table and saw him walking toward the dance floor, a gorgeous blonde on his arm. She had a cool elegance, and an aura of sensuality that one would expect to find in a woman with Stephen Dalheurst. Jessica felt a strange pang of jealousy. Jealousy? *Why should I be jealous?* she asked herself.

She watched his hand sliding suggestively across that slim elegant back and felt the heat rising under her own skin. She knew that touch, and the memory of it made her legs feel weak.

Suddenly she needed air. She had had far too much to drink, and the atmosphere in the bar was getting thick and heavy. She had to get out. She jumped from her chair and, forcing her way through the crowd of people, made her way to the door.

Once on the sidewalk she gasped for air, inhaling the cold frosty night, its biting chill numbing her lungs. She had left her jacket inside, but she didn't even notice the cold. It numbed not only her body, but her brain as well. It kept her from thinking about Stephen's hands roaming over the willowy blonde in the bar.

Suddenly Bill was beside her.

"Are you all right, Jessica?" Concern was written in the frown on his face.

"Yes, I'm fine. . . . I think I must have had too much to drink that's all."

"It was getting pretty stuffy in there. I was starting to feel a little sick myself." Always the gentleman, Jessica thought. Bill would never think of making her feel like a fool; such a nice, nice man. "Let me get your wrap, though. It's too cold for you to be out here without it." He rushed inside to get her coat, making her aware of how cold it really was. When he returned, she was grateful for the warmth of the coat and his arm around her.

"I think I'd like to go home now, if you don't mind, Bill."

"Of course." She could tell he was disappointed, but being a gentleman, he tried not to let it show. "I'll go tell the others good-bye."

"No. Bill, I didn't mean you had to leave. I'll just grab a cab."

"Don't be silly, Jessica. I'll take you home."

"Really," she insisted, "there's no need for that. I take cabs all the time. Please, I want you to stay and have a good time."

From the shadowy doorway of the bar Stephen stepped into the light of the sidewalk. Not even looking at Jessica, Stephen said, "Don't worry about her, Bill. I'll make sure she gets home all right." Bill was ready to protest this rude intrusion when Stephen, aware of Bill's thoughts, continued. "I need to talk to her about some business, if you don't mind, old buddy." Bill looked at Jessica for her reaction, but the alcohol and the cold had numbed her senses to the point where she could not react at all.

"All right, I guess. Is that okay with you, Jessica?" Bill was genuinely concerned about her, and his ego was a little bit bruised as well, but he was too nice a guy to create a scene over it. Before Jessica could break out of her stunned silence to respond, Stephen had grabbed her elbow and was moving away from Bill. She looked back over her shoulder at him standing on the sidewalk, abandoned and confused, cowboy hat clutched tightly in his hands.

"Bill," she called. "Thank you. I had a wonderf—" Stephen dragged her forcefully across the street, making it impossible to finish her thanks to Bill. "You're hurting my elbow. Where are you taking me?"

Stephen didn't answer, but held her arm even tighter, pulling her with him down the street into a parking lot, where he unlocked the door to his Jaguar and thrust her into the front seat. She wanted to resist his brutal force, but she was too weak from the alcohol to do much of anything.

He positioned himself behind the wheel, started the engine, and backed the car out of the lot.

"That was a terribly rude thing you did to Bill back there," she accused.

"Do you really care?" he drawled.

"Care? Of course, I care." The look on Stephen's face was skeptical. "You don't believe me?"

"No." He watched the traffic light until it turned green, then drove through the intersection, maneuvering the high-performance vehicle around street revelers and parked cars.

"Bill is a kind man." The disbelieving smugness in Stephen's expression prompted her to defend her date.

"Yes, he is," Stephen said, but the amused smile never left his face.

"And a gentleman."

"Yes, he is."

"Which is something you most definitely are not!" she accused. Who did he think he was, whisking her away from her date, dragging her to his car, and then insulting Bill in front of her? But then, had she been thinking more rationally, she would have realized that Stephen had said nothing about Bill that could be considered an insult.

"Bill means nothing to you, and you know it." Stephen's voice was so self-assured, so confident in its indisputable knowledge.

"Oh? And what makes you so sure of that?" she countered.

"I saw you dancing with him." He had been watching her dancing with Bill! The disclosure jolted her. She suddenly felt vulnerable and unprotected. But then, so what? What could her dancing with Bill possibly have revealed?

"And?" she asked sarcastically.

"And"—he drawled—"I know you felt nothing." Before she could find words to express her anger, he continued. "You didn't caress his neck with your hand. You didn't lean closer to him when he slid his hand across your back. Oh, you were both very polished dancers, I must admit that. Very accomplished and graceful. But I know emotion when I see it, Jessica. And you felt nothing." She was seething inside, bristling with righteous anger at this penetrating attack on her personal feelings. Although what he said about her feelings toward Bill was probably true, she refused to admit it.

Stephen had pulled the car over to the curb and turned off the engine. But Jessica, blinded by anger, did not notice. She pivoted in her seat, ready to attack him with vindictive zeal, when his mouth descended on her open lips. Suddenly the blaze of anger in her died, leaving a seething fire of desire growing in its place. The alcohol, while numbing her powers of resistance, had at the same time awakened her acute sense of touch. The feel of his lips on hers warmed and electrified her entire body. It was not a soft kiss, but a demanding one, full of urgency and a desperate, primitive need. His arms were clamped around her tightly, squeezing the breath out of her.

Before she lost all the air in her lungs, he released her, but only long enough to grasp her underneath her arms, pulling her behind the steering wheel onto his lap. He pulled the lever under the seat to move it back a couple of inches. Before she could protest, he once again invaded her mouth, this time probing deeper and deeper, caressing her lips and teeth with his tongue. She responded completely. The attack on her senses, so long deprived of stimulation, left her immune to reason, powerless to resist his touch. She was blind with a yearning she had not felt in years.

When his mouth left hers, she whispered "no" and pulled him down to meet her own urgent need. His mouth played across her face, causing her breath to quicken. He gently bit the lobe of her ear, sending a shiver to the base of her spine. Trailing his kisses down her neck, his tongue in the sensitive hollow of her throat, he heard her moan softly, further kindling his own need to demand more of her.

"Jessie—" But he was unable to finish as her mouth moved aggressively toward his, her hunger for his kisses

56

driving all reason from her mind. His right hand slid up from her waist and cupped her breast, his thumb moving back and forth across the nipple, hardening it to a peak. Loving the feel of his hands on her body, she trailed her own hand down his neck and across the broad expanse of his shirt-covered chest.

He began unfastening the buttons of her crepe blouse, his fingers slipping inside after each button opened. She pressed herself more tightly against him, needing his touch to satisfy the ache she had carried for seven years. "Touch me, Stephen. Please touch me." Her own hands were finding their way to the buttons of his shirt, frantically unfastening them and reaching inside to curl her fingers in the tightly woven hair of his chest.

"Let me love you, Jessie." Her head fell back across his left shoulder as his mouth and tongue circled her now exposed breasts.

"Yes, Stephen. Love me," she breathed. All fear of him vanished; and need superseded all doubts and cares. He pushed her skirt out of the way, and his right hand kneaded its way up her leg, his fingers caressing the inner thigh. Her hips arched toward his fingers, the fire inside her completely out of control. Her need was so great, she felt if it were not satisfied, something inside her would explode.

"You're still mine . . . even after all these years." It was said in the heat of passion, but his words penetrated into the deep recesses of her brain, jolting her memories awake. A siren shrieked from somewhere inside her, sending out subtle warning signals. Alerting her to some imminent danger. She had been falling, falling into Stephen's snare, and now she knew she had to crawl back out of the deep and fiery crevasse before she was burned alive. The alcohol seemed to evaporate through her pores as the alarm blared at full blast now.

She pushed away from him, but his arms attempted to hold her tightly to his body.

"Stephen," she yelled as she pushed against his chest, straining to reach the other seat. "No!"

"No? What do you mean, 'no'?" He was confused and agitated by her sudden brusque change.

"Just stop, Stephen. I want you to stop. . . . I want you to take me home." She stared straight ahead out the front window, unable to face the man who, only a moment before, had filled her with a burning need such as she had never felt before.

"What are you trying to do to me?" he hissed. She could feel the dangerous heat from his eyes, and his breath was hot and angry. But it didn't matter what he said or thought now. She despised him.

You're mine now, Jessie. You'll always be mine. She wanted to scream at him, to throw her fists into his face! Did he think he could just walk back into her life after seven years and take up where he left off? What would he do after she let him make love to her? Would he just walk out of her life for another seven years?

When he spoke, his voice was low and thick, the sound of it grating on the raw edges of her nerves. "I thought you might be tough-skinned, Jessica, but I never would have thought you were a tease." The intense heat in his voice fanned the flames of her anger. "There's another word I could put in front of *tease* if *I* wasn't a gentleman."

His emphasis on the word *I* bolted her upright in her seat. "Gentleman! You are anything *but* a gentleman!" She was shouting now, and it felt good. It released the anger and tension and fiery emotions boiling inside her.

"And you are certainly one to talk about teasing!" As soon as she had said it, she wished she could have taken it back.

"What are you talking about?" He pounced upon her accusation with a low growl.

Why did I have to open my big, stupid mouth? Get hold of yourself, Jessica. Don't let him know how he hurt you years ago, how he destroyed any chance of your finding happiness with another man.

"Nothing," she whispered, the fight in her now completely dissipated. "Just take me home . . . please." She turned to look at his face. The passion and the fire were gone from those deep chocolate eyes. They were now two hard, brown stones, unpolished and silent, chiseled into his rigid and unfathomable expression. Without a word he thrust the car into drive and sped carelessly through the streets, screaming through traffic, his marble profile fixed on the road ahead. He pulled sharply into the curb in front of Jessica's town house. She had not given him the address, but she wasn't about to ask him how he knew where she lived. She didn't really care. She was quickly learning that if Stephen Dalheurst wanted something, nothing would be an obstacle to his obtaining it. Without a word from either of them she jumped from the car and ran up the stairs of her brownstone.

Though she didn't turn around, she knew he was still sitting there watching her. She entered the house and closed the door behind her, leaning all of her weight against it. She didn't bother turning on the light. Nothing could illuminate the cavernous darkness that seemed to swallow her mind and body.

CHAPTER FOUR

When she awoke the following morning, Jessica's head was reeling from the alcohol she had consumed and the bitter, emotional confrontation with Stephen. She wasn't accustomed to drinking, so she blamed most of her headache on that. She didn't want to admit that Stephen could still upset her this much. She didn't want to think about last night.

As she bustled around her small, efficient kitchen, shaking coffee grounds into the filter paper and adding water to the automatic drip pot, the memories of the previous night continued to plague her. Why had she responded to him the way she had? It wasn't simply a matter of letting him kiss her. She had kissed him back! She had wanted to feel his body next to hers. She had wanted him to make love to her. The thought of it even now, as she leaned against the kitchen counter, caused an uneasy fluttering in her stomach. Why was she so physically drawn to him? It was finally an offer of admittance; it was more than a mere attraction. She was consumed with desire for him—she could no longer deny it. But why? He was everything she despised in a man: arrogant, unfeeling, power-hungry, domineering. He was a selfish, arrogant boor who twisted the emotions and lives of everyone around him.

Maybe the attraction was based solely upon a memory. Her love for him as a young girl had obviously meant nothing to him, whereas it had meant . . . everything—yes, everything—to her. But perhaps over the past seven years she had unwittingly inflated his importance in her mind by endowing him with undesirable characteristics, and by consciously striving to push his image from her thoughts. And had she embellished a purely physical moment seven years ago with more than was actually there? It was possible, she reluctantly admitted. But he had seemed so sincere and emotionally involved himself. *You'll always be mine.* His words echoed through the canyons of her mind. She saw him standing on the cliff, the sky blue and cloudless with the invigoratingly raw air of fall, his honey-spun hair tousled and gleaming. His eyes, amber in the autumn light, had spoken of tenderness—of love. There had been definitely something more there than just a purely physical encounter. There had to have been!

But he was different now. He wasn't the same gentle man she had loved seven years ago. This Stephen Dalheurst was cold and hard and cruel. She did not want to feel anything for this reprehensible person. She detested him, in fact, and felt that he was using her. She wasn't sure why, but she was certain that he was using her for some personal gain. Her world, all neatly tied up with ribbons and tape, was being shredded by Stephen's constant presence in her life. She had worked too hard to organize her life for it to fall apart now. She would have to make sure that she stayed away from him, and that he stayed away from her.

On Saturday afternoon Bill called to make sure that she had made it home all right. He seemed vaguely disturbed by Stephen's insistence on driving her home, but he veiled his hurt and jealousy in concern for Jessica.

"I really want to apologize for not taking you home," he said.

"There's no need to apologize, Bill. I wanted you to stay with the rest of the group. Besides, I made it home just fine." Her casual tone eased his concern somewhat and the conversation moved away from the tense scene of the night before.

"Could you have dinner with me tonight, Jessica?"

"Bill, if you're still feeling bad about last night, there's really no need—"

"No! I just thought maybe you'd like to go out." His voice held a youthful eagerness that she had not heard in him before. She hated to disappoint him, but she simply couldn't bear the thought of feigning a good time when her mind was still reeling from the disastrous turn of events last night.

"I'm sorry, Bill, but I have several things I need to do here. Maybe some other time." She cringed at the silence that answered her.

"Sure, Jessica. Okay. . . . Maybe we'll have lunch sometime next week."

"That would be nice," she lied. He was such a nice man, she thought again. But after last night, her feelings for him—for any man—had turned sour.

She moved through the following week in a daze. She went to work each day, mechanically checking stock prices, calling clients, placing spread orders and puts and calls, evaluating accounts, and reading up on the latest regulations from the Securities and Exchange Commission and the Federal Reserve Board.

Somehow she never got around to having that discussion with Mr. Caldwell about Stephen's account. She told herself that she didn't want to antagonize her boss and jeopardize her position with the firm. She refused to admit that there might be another reason.

After having been asked several days in a row, Jessica finally agreed to have lunch with Bill on Thursday. They had to wait about ten minutes for a table, but once they were seated, the food came quickly.

"I guess you're wondering why I've asked you here," Bill said, chuckling as they waited for their bowls of steaming chili to cool.

"I assumed it was the fact that I'm dynamite company," Jessica teased.

"It is, it is." Bill was quick to agree. "But I've decided that the only way to convince you to go to lunch with me is under the ruse of business."

"That's not true, Bill. I really have been busy this week," she insisted.

"I know you have. And this isn't a trick. I really do need some advice."

"Professional?"

Bill nodded his head.

"Okay, shoot." Jessica was more than happy to keep the conversation on a business level. Her nerves couldn't handle anymore personal confrontations.

"I feel that my life is becoming very dull and I want to spice it up a little bit." He twitched his eyebrows comically like Groucho Marx, indicating that the spice might include her. But when she didn't react to the hidden meaning, he qualified the statement by saying, "I thought I'd start with my investments."

"What did you have in mind?" she asked, refusing to acknowledge his previous remark about spicing up his life.

"Well, I was thinking about buying some stocks on margin or maybe playing around with some options. But I'm afraid I don't know much about either." Jessica noticed that Bill didn't seem in the least embarrassed at needing advice from a woman. That was one of the characteristics she especially liked about him: He was secure enough in his own manhood that he was able to treat a woman as an equal. No male ego problems here, she reflected.

"Well," she began. "When you buy stock on margin, you pay only a portion of the total cost, and your broker extends credit to you on the balance. A credit charge is made monthly to your account on the amount you borrow. The amount you have to put up is, of course, determined by the Fed."

"What is that amount?" Bill asked between spoonfuls of chili.

"Right now, it's fifty percent. But that could change at any time."

Bill was mulling over some figures of his cash already invested when Jessica added, "You know, Bill, you've got enough invested now that we could start up a ready asset trust for you. We would just keep all of your holdings in house, and that would give you more than enough to qualify for a margin account."

"Okay," he agreed. "That sounds like a pretty good idea. But another thing is— Well, you remember last year, before you were my broker, when I invested in some put options?"

Jessica nodded.

"That was a total disaster. I lost a lot of money on that deal. Quite a few people I know make money on options, but I'm still a little shaky about them. What do you think?"

"Well," Jessica explained, "with the economic situation the way it is right now, I wouldn't recommend put options. However, you might try some call options as a way to hedge certain securities against a possible decline in market value."

Jessica had always had an analytical mind. She enrolled in pre-law classes at the university and intended to go to law school following graduation. But after the death of her parents and brother, the idea of following in her father's footsteps no longer held any attraction for her. Instead, she threw her energies into studying business, maintaining a 4.0 average throughout the last three years of college.

"The recession," Bill was saying. "That's another thing that worries me about investing too heavily in the market. Don't let your food get cold, Jessica."

"No, I won't." She took several bites of the now luke-warm chili. It was no longer hot, but it still tasted delicious. She ate a couple of crackers and drank half her coffee before continuing.

"Actually, Bill, periods of recession provide attractive opportunities for investing in equities."

"That's probably true. I know that, as far as private businesses go, times of recession have usually been periods during which they rebuild their liquidity. They in effect create a foundation for the next expansion."

Jessica nodded as she took another bite of chili. "I

know. That's why we recommend that investors become increasingly aggressive in using periods of market weakness to establish or to build long-term investment positions in equities." She watched silently as the waitress refilled her cup of coffee. "You see, as interest rates decline, equities become increasingly attractive in relation to alternative fixed-income investments."

"Well," he admitted, "I do feel much better after talking to you. Maybe we should set up that ready asset account. Will you handle that for me?" He folded his napkin and set it beside his plate. Jessica did the same.

"Sure, I'll take care of it for you." She watched Bill's face as it changed from pleasant complacency to eager anticipation.

"Why don't we go out to dinner tomorrow night? To pay for your services," he quickly added.

"Your commissions will pay for my services, Bill." Jessica was smiling, hoping he wouldn't push her for a commitment.

"Well, I'm sure we could find another excuse to go out to dinner." He was smiling, too, leaning toward her with a conspiratorial grin.

"Maybe some other time, Bill. But thank you anyway." Poor Bill. She didn't want to hurt his feelings. But she wanted to get her life back on an even keel, back to the sanctity of uninvolvement.

"That's what you said last weekend. You know, a guy could get a complex from your rejections." His comment was uttered in jest, but Jessica noted a hint of real hurt in his tone. He was scrutinizing her with a questioning look on his face, and she wondered if he surmised that Stephen Dalheurst had anything to do with her declining the invitation.

She didn't have to surmise for long; Bill's next comment revealed his thoughts.

"Heard anything from Stephen this week?" His expression was an obvious, strained attempt at nonchalance, but she had a hard time containing that same casual look when she spoke.

"No." Just the mention of his name was enough to make her pulse race and her body heat rise. "How do you and . . . Stephen know each other?" She threw the ball into Bill's court, hoping to switch the conversation away from herself.

"We went to Harvard together. We were in the same fraternity and, of course, being from the same city brought all of the Chicagoans closer together. But I've only seen him a few times since we graduated." His tone revealed that the few times he had seen him were enough.

"Well, I think he's been in Europe for the last several years," she shrugged, feigning disinterest.

"That's true. But he's back and forth. He has several businesses in this country, too, you know."

She looked surprised. "No, I didn't know." In fact, she knew very little about him. "I really haven't kept up with him—other than what I read occasionally in the papers." She had seen his name blazed across the newspapers in a continuous stream of scandalous escapades. "I guess some people like to read that smut. I don't." She wasn't aware of the scowl on her face at the thought of what those articles contained.

"Oh, I don't know. It's kind of fun wallowing in all the juicy details. He has achieved a certain amount of fame through his notorious love affairs, hasn't he?"

How did they get on the topic of Stephen's love affairs?

Surely there was something more to the man than his disgusting sex life.

"Stephen Dalheurst gave new meaning to the term *filthy rich*," Jessica retorted. Her tone clearly implied that she was tired of this discussion.

Bill sighed heavily and waved to the waitress to bring the check. The walk back to her office was mostly silent, punctuated now and then by stilted, trivial conversation.

Jessica was relieved that she hadn't heard anything from Stephen since last Friday night. Yet, at the same time, she found herself wondering what he was doing. She told herself it didn't matter, but she wondered all the same.

She was glad she had declined Bill's invitation for Friday night, wanting instead a quiet weekend to herself to do laundry and clean her town house.

She could easily have afforded a housekeeper, but she preferred to take care of it herself. She liked a simplified existence. Her house was conveniently located and tastefully decorated, but she kept it simple, without expensive furnishings.

With Benchcrest it was different. She supplied Señor and Señora Esclanada with all the money they needed to keep the estate in perfect shape. Jessica also included in every paycheck a considerable bonus to the couple for remaining so loyal and trustworthy. She often wondered what would happen to the place without their loving care. She would like to see them again. It had been so long since she had sat down at the large wooden table in the kitchen and had a heart-to-heart chat with Rosita. She missed them. But if she saw them, it would have to be at Benchcrest, and she could not make herself go there, even for a visit.

On Friday night Jessica tackled her week's worth of laundry. Though unpretentious, her town house had ample space for a separate laundry room. By ten o'clock she had washed, folded, and pressed everything she would need for the next week.

Saturday and Sunday were equally uneventful. On Saturday she paid some bills and looked over a list of needed repairs for Benchcrest, approving each item and writing the corresponding check for the job. On Sunday she shopped for groceries and supplies for the next week.

Lying in bed Sunday night, she wondered why she couldn't sleep. The weekend had gone just as she had planned—easy and undemanding, like ninety percent of her weekends. So why did she feel so empty? She had enjoyed her undemanding schedule and quiet life before, but now she felt as if something were missing, as if there were no meaning or joy to her life. But then that was absurd, she told herself. She had her job, which she loved. She had her town house and Benchcrest to take care of. If she wanted companionship, she had Bill. What more could she want?

The hollow ache inside her kept her awake for long hours before she finally drifted off into a fitful, dream-filled sleep.

Her days were filled with emptiness, an emptiness she had trouble explaining away. Each night she would lie awake in her bed, which seemed to grow heavier and heavier with the weight of loneliness.

The monotony of her days ended the following Wednesday afternoon, but the dread that took its place made Jessica realize that she was better off with the emptiness.

She was heading out the door of the office. It had been a long day, and she was ready to get home and soak in a hot, bubbly tub. Her hand was pushing the door open when Mr. Caldwell stopped her.

"Jessica. I'm glad I caught you before you left. My wife and I are having a little party Saturday night and we'd like you to come."

Jessica couldn't have been more surprised. She had never been invited to a party at the Caldwells' before. Why were they inviting her? "Is it an office party?" she asked, a feeling of unease creeping between her shoulder blades.

"No," he smiled. "That's why I didn't mention it earlier in the day. I didn't want to hurt the others' feelings by letting them know that some of the staff were invited and some not." Noticing her confused frown, he continued. "It's a party for some of our biggest investors, and . . . well, since you handle some of the larger accounts, I thought you should be there."

"Mr. Caldwell," she began cautiously, "is Stephen Dalheurst going to be there?"

"Why, yes. . . . I believe he is." Bob Caldwell's attempt at nonchalance was totally unbelievable. She knew that Stephen had put him up to this. After all, she had seen how convincing he had been with Caldwell before. But she was not going to let him manipulate her that way. No way!

"Mr. Caldwell, I've been meaning to talk to you about Stephen's account. I don't think . . . I really don't want—"

"Jessica." Mr. Caldwell placed his hand on her shoulder in a sympathetic, fatherly fashion. "I know all about it. Stephen told me. You really don't need to worry about that."

"He told you!" She was shocked. She couldn't believe that Stephen was actually so cruel as to tell her most intimate secrets to her boss. There must be some mistake. "What—what exactly did he tell you, Mr. Caldwell?" She tried to conceal the shaking of her hands by stuffing them into her coat pocket. It was suddenly so warm in the office, she was beginning to perspire under the bulky coat.

"Well, he told me that you would probably try to talk me into giving his account to someone else because you once gave him a tip in the market that cost him thousands of dollars in a loss."

"What!" She was outraged.

"It's really nothing to be ashamed about." He sat on the edge of the receptionist's vacated desk, his arms folded in front of him. "It happens to all of us at one time or another." Ignoring Jessica's gaping mouth, he chuckled at some private joke. "I remember once I sold some gold options for a guy who was just beginning to invest in the market. The stock took a dive, and the guy lost all of his money. I turned him off to the stock market forever. To this day he has never put another dime in the market. So you see, it's really nothing to worry about. The fact that Stephen has faith in your judgment should assure you of that."

"Mr. Caldwell," Jessica began, fuming inside but maintaining her cool composure on the outside, "I'm afraid that Stephen has given you the wrong information—"

"Jessica." The voice had a definitive ring to it.

"But, Mr. Caldwell," she insisted.

"Jessica, I do not want to lose this account." There was a finality in his voice that kept her from opening her mouth again. When he noticed that she was not going to

71

argue anymore, he smiled. "I'll see you Saturday night. Right?"

She nodded passively.

"Good. Have a nice evening and I'll see you tomorrow."

She watched him turn and walk into his office, closing the door behind him, before she stepped out into the frosty night air.

CHAPTER FIVE

Jessica stepped from the cab, making sure the swaying length of her skirt did not catch in the door before she closed it. She paid the driver and watched him as he drove out of the circular drive onto the main road, then sighed heavily, wishing she were anywhere but here. She craned her neck and looked up at the high-rise apartment building. From this vantage point she had a fish-eye view of its three-leaf-clover shape. Students of architecture found Chicago a treasure house. The buildings of the city did not aim primarily for utilitarian practicality, nor did they aim for mere attractiveness: they aimed for greatness. And some, like this Lake Point Tower apartment complex had attained just that.

Jessica stepped through the glass-plated doors into the outer lobby. Here she was obstructed from entering farther by a uniformed security guard. He had a weathered look, years of boredom and disillusionment inscribed in his haggard expression. He made no attempt to be discreet as he flipped through the papers on his desk, checking her name against the list provided by the Caldwells. She secretly hoped that her name would not be on the list, but her hopes were dashed when he looked at her resentfully and pushed open the second pair of doors for her to enter the inner lobby. In no hurry to arrive, she walked to the elevator slowly. She had been dreading this social event for three days, but decided that she would rather prolong the dread than have to actually face Stephen. At the thought of him her heart began beating too rapidly, and she unconsciously smoothed her skirt and touched her hair to make sure it was still in place.

Jessica had chosen her outfit for the evening with Stephen in mind. She had picked a long royal blue silk wrapskirt and a white silk blouse with a flower at the throat. She wanted to wear something that would not elicit any lascivious remarks from him—not that he was the type to make lewd comments. But she was taking no chances. However, as she walked past a large mirror on the way to the elevator, she noticed with chagrin that when she walked, a substantial portion of her left calf and thigh showed, and that the sheerness of her blouse probably revealed more than a plunging neckline would have. And yet—not for the first time—she wondered if he would be pleased with the way she looked.

"Hi, Jessica." Hastily turning from the mirror, Jessica saw Roger Haskell, one of the brokers from the office, walking toward her with his date. "I see you were one of the chosen ones too," he said with a laugh. "This is Cindy. Cindy, Jessica Benchley."

Jessica and Cindy nodded hello to each other.

They stepped into the elevator, and Roger punched the button for the fifteenth floor. "Do you believe this?" He seemed as shocked by the invitation as Jessica had been. "I mean, God Almighty inviting *us* to *his* place. We must have done something right."

Jessica mumbled her agreement, her nerves frayed and weak. As the elevator rose she watched the floor numbers light up and felt an impending sense of doom. Why did she have to be here when, instead, she could be home, safe and secure in her own quiet desperation?

The party was in full swing when they entered the apartment. Laughter and confused noise greeted them at the door. Jessica was slightly relieved at the large number of people. At least in a crowd there was always the chance to get lost. She noticed Bob Caldwell trying to make his way to the door.

"Jessica, hello." Mr. Caldwell extended his hand. "I'm so glad you could make it," he added, as if he had any doubt that she would. "What would you like to drink?"

"Oh, it doesn't matter."

"We have a little of everything."

"I'll have some wine, then, please." She really didn't want anything to drink. She wanted to remain levelheaded throughout the evening. She certainly didn't want a repeat of St. Patty's Day. But at least a glass in her hand would give her something to do.

"Stephen's around here somewhere." Mr. Caldwell returned with her glass of wine. "I think you know several of the people here. And—oh, here comes my wife. Joanne, you remember Jessica Benchley, don't you? Jessica, my wife, Joanne."

"Yes," Jessica said, smiling. "We met at the office Christmas party a couple of years ago. How are you?"

"I'm fine, and Bob tells me you're the best account executive in the office."

"No, I don't think so," Jessica replied humbly, but was inwardly pleased that Mrs. Caldwell would have heard about her achievements.

"Don't be modest. It's—Oh, dear, I see someone signaling me from the kitchen. I had better see what the problem is."

"Do you need some help?" Jessica asked eagerly.

"No, dear. You just mingle and have a good time." Jessica was disappointed. She wanted an excuse to stay away from Stephen, and helping in the kitchen would have been a perfect one.

She looked around the room. The view from the apartment was spectacular. Wraparound windows allowed a panoramic vista of the lake from one side and downtown Chicago from the other. Sounds of laughter and indistinct conversations floated through the spacious apartment. There were small groups of people seated on couches and chairs by the fireplace; others were standing by the bar and by the buffet table, which was loaded with appetizers.

The air smelled heavily of tobacco smoke, punctuated by the sweet fragrance of women's perfume. Jessica noticed people locked in conversation and wished that she could find someone to whom to attach herself, someone other than Stephen. Maybe Roger and his date, Cindy. She and Roger had never had much to talk about at the office, but at least he and Cindy would make her feel less alone.

She was just turning around to look for them when her eyes collided with Stephen's.

"Looking for me?" he asked smiling, an expression of complacency on his face. He was standing not more than two feet away. His eyes, filled with wicked amusement, trailed seductively over her blouse and skirt, taking in every curve of her body.

He looked stunning. His light golden hair was a dramatic contrast to the dark suit he wore. He was made to wear fine clothes, Jessica noticed. His broad shoulders and slim waist and hips provided the perfect frame for designer cuts. Looking at him, she had to make a conscious effort to control her breathing.

"As a matter of fact, I wasn't," she replied coolly, the smugness in his expression forcing her to retain her composure.

"You look ravishing tonight." His eyes again swept across her body.

"Well, for a person who seems to enjoy ravishing other people, I can hardly take that as a compliment."

He laughed away her retort. "Let's go get something to drink."

"Stephen, I'd really rather not—"

He grabbed her arm at the elbow and pulled her beside him. Her hand was placed in the crook of his arm, his other hand on top of hers. "See? Isn't that easy?" He smiled. They were walking through the crowd, making their way to the bar. Occasionally Stephen would stop and say hello to someone they passed. He would introduce Jessica, and she would have to make an effort to look as though she were enjoying herself. She felt as if he were parading her around to make sure that everyone saw them together, that everyone knew that—at least for the evening—she belonged to him. She tried once to pull her arm from his, but his elbow dug into his side, thwarting her escape. Looking at her glum expression, he leaned his face close to her ear. "Have you always worn a hair shirt, Jessica, or is it just when I'm around that you put it on?"

At that moment Jessica would have given anything to be able to wipe that insolent grin from his face.

"I do not wear a hair shirt," she hissed.

"Then why do you punish yourself so?" He was still whispering, his face close to hers. "This is a party. You're supposed to have fun."

"I do not like to be tricked into going to parties—or anywhere else, for that matter."

"Tricked?" His look was one of feigned innocence.

"Don't play innocent with me, Stephen. I know what you told Mr. Caldwell about me and I think it was a low-down, sneaky, rotten, despicable thing to do." She was trying once again, without success, to pull her arm free of his.

"Oh, come on," he smiled. "Can't you take a joke?"

"I can take a joke when it's funny. That was not. I don't know what it is you want from me, Stephen, but lying about me is not the way to get it."

"What is the way to get it, Jessie?" At the serious suggestiveness in his tone she felt a shudder in her loins.

"Please let me go," she cried desperately. "I have to get some air."

"Come on. I know just the place."

Before she could protest, he was pulling her through the crowd, picking up her wrap, and pushing her out the door in front of him.

There were other people on the elevator, so she was unable to argue with him about where he was taking her. They stepped off the elevator at the third floor. He pulled her down a hallway through some double glass doors. Suddenly they were in the middle of a park—a park three stories above the street. She could see a narrow path leading through a small wooded area; a circular pond with

78

winter-feathered ducks resting on its tranquil surface; and a large, now empty, swimming pool with a surrounding deck.

"I didn't know this was here." She marveled at the idea of building a park on the third floor of a high rise.

"The wall that goes around the apartment building keeps out intruders. The only way into the building is past that grisly-faced guard in the lobby."

"This is really nice. The tenants have their own private park."

"Come on." Stephen led her past the swimming pool and toward the clump of trees. The moon was full, and its white light shimmered across the surface of the pond where the ducks swam in silence. Only a few patches of snow remained, mostly in covered shady niches hidden from the sun. The air was cold and crisp; it was just the kind of clear night that seemed to heighten one's senses. Jessica wanted to see what the park looked like, but she wasn't sure that she wanted Stephen showing it to her.

"All I wanted was some fresh air. I'm ready to go back now." She had turned back toward the building.

"What are you afraid of, Jessica?" The challenge in his voice and eyes brought a fiery spark to her eyes. She raised her head higher, tilting her chin outward. Her eyes blazed in acceptance of the challenge.

"I am not afraid of anything." She would show him. She turned around and started back down the path through the trees, staying at least a foot ahead of him.

"You want to slow down?" His hand reached out to grasp her elbow. "This isn't a race." She grudgingly slowed her pace to walk beside him. "So tell me." His arm slipped around her shoulder. "What have you been doing the last couple of weeks?"

"Working."

"Just working?" His tone was now polite and casually indifferent.

"Just working."

"How's Bill?"

"Bill is fine. What is this, the third degree?"

"Look, I'm just trying to make conversation. You seem to be a little uptight."

"I am not uptight," she insisted.

"Well, I hope nothing is wrong with your hands then. You certainly seem to be wringing them nervously."

"All right, Stephen." She didn't want to compete with his sarcasm anymore. It was too much of a drain on her energy. Besides, she couldn't win anyway. "So you tell me. What have *you* been doing the last couple of weeks? See, I can make idle conversation too."

"Well, let's see, I went to New York on business . . . and to visit my mother."

"Your mother lives in New York now?"

"Yes. She has a suite in one of my hotels."

"She lives in a hotel!" Jessica was appalled. Couldn't Stephen even see fit to buy his own mother a house?

"She likes it, Jessica. After my father died, she didn't want the big house, so she moved into the hotel. She has lots of friends," he insisted, noting the indignant look on her face. "They go to all the Broadway shows, restaurants, museums." He was quiet for a moment, but Jessica sensed that he had something more to say. "It took her a long time to get over him—my father—and I'm just glad she's finally happy."

"Yes, I was fairly young when he died, but I remember how depressed she was for a long time. I'm glad she's happy now too." She looked at Stephen and noticed that he was staring off into the distance. She didn't think that he had heard her at all.

"She really loved him." He was speaking as if to himself. "He was much older than she was, but they had a relationship you don't find very often anymore."

Jessica was startled at his ability to see real love. She didn't think he even knew what the word meant. When he turned to her and put his arms around her waist, she realized that she had been staring at him.

"Some relationships are just meant to be, I guess." His voice was low; his eyes like powerful magnets, pulling her into their depths.

"I guess so," she said, hypnotized by the smoldering look in his eyes and the musky male scent of him. But her hands remained on his chest, putting a certain distance between them.

"I'm leaving for Europe tomorrow," he announced. "I won't be back for a couple of weeks." It was another challenge, and Jessica found herself unable to resist it. She could feel the play of muscles under his chest and shoulders. As his lips zeroed in on hers her arms instinctively circled his neck. The kiss was a long, drugging one, their mouths fusing together in a burning, silent embrace. She leaned her head to the side, resting it slightly on his shoulder. His tongue burrowed deep into her mouth, and her own tongue responded. She didn't want this to happen, but she could not escape it. The needs and longings that she had kept buried for so many years would not be suppressed any longer. His physical power over her was too strong, and she knew she could no longer resist. His hand trailed down her back, resting on her hips and pulling them tighter against his frame.

"Oh, sorry." The apology pierced the cool night air.

"Roger! Cindy!" Jessica exclaimed, jumping out of Stephen's arms.

"We didn't mean to interrupt anything," Roger apologized. "We just wanted to look around this park. Do you believe this?" he exclaimed, using his favorite sentence. "Here we are, three stories above Lake Shore Drive—in a park!"

A moment ago, Jessica did not want to escape the arms of Stephen Dalheurst. Now she wanted nothing more than to flee. Once again, she had been drugged by his kiss, by his touch, by him. It infuriated her that she had no more willpower than that, but she had a strangely mixed reaction to Roger's interruption: half relief and half annoyance.

"It's getting cold. I think I'll go back in now." Roger and Cindy had walked on down the path.

Stephen grabbed her elbow, his voice impatient and taunting. "Is that what you want, or what you think you should do?"

She hoped he did not notice her hesitation. "It's what I want."

"Liar."

Before she could deny the accusation, his hand clasped the back of her neck, his mouth bruising her lips in a long, searing, punishing kiss. "Just something to remember me by while I'm gone." His voice was mocking, but his eyes held a dark threat.

Once out of his arms Jessica felt the chill night air attack her vulnerable nerves. She lifted the back of her hand to her mouth, her lips swollen and tender. She could not tear her eyes away from his face; his penetrating stare bore holes into her weakening facade.

Remember him? She would never forget him.

* * *

The following week was extremely hectic. Due to the devaluation of the dollar on the international market, the stock market plummeted. Panicked buyers wanted to sell, and the more daring investors wanted to buy while prices were so low. Jessica had little time to think of Stephen during the day. Only at night did she feel the hollow ache inside her; the emptiness and the loneliness.

At noon on Wednesday she was picking up her coat off the back of her chair when a friend stopped by the office.

"Jessica, hi."

"Hi, Angela. I haven't seen you in a while. What have you been up to?"

"Oh," Angela smiled wickedly. "I've been busy—if you know what I mean."

"Hmm." Angela made no secret of her lust for life and for the opposite sex. Since their days together in college, Jessica had been shocked, but enthralled, by the girl's sex life. Angela was much shorter than Jessica, with fair skin and golden hair. Rounded and full in all the right places, she had a blatant voluptuousness about her features that few men failed to notice.

Though their views on life differed drastically, they had been close friends for many years.

"But I understand you've been pretty busy yourself." There was a significance in Angela's laugh that Jessica failed to decipher.

"Yes, I have," Jessica answered honestly. "The market's going crazy these days."

"That wasn't what I was referring to," Angela drawled. "I've just heard some very interesting news about you."

"Oh?" Jessica was slipping her arms into the sleeves of her coat. "I'm going to lunch. You want to go?"

"Yes," Angela agreed readily. "I have some shopping to do at Water Tower, so can we eat there?"

"Sure." Jessica buttoned her coat, and the two women left the office and headed up Wacker toward Michigan Avenue. It was quite a walk to the shopping complex known as Water Tower Place, but the weather had warmed considerably, so Jessica figured it would be a pleasant diversion for lunch.

"So are you going to fill me in or not?" Angela asked impatiently.

"I don't know what you're talking about." Jessica was genuinely baffled.

"You and Stephen Dalheurst, silly." Angela was annoyed at Jessica's excessive reticence.

"What!" Jessica was incredulous.

"Don't play coy with me, Jessica. You know I'll dig it out of you one way or another."

"I can't imagine what you've heard, Angela, but I'm shocked at you—believing in idle gossip."

The two women looked at each other and burst out laughing like a couple of adolescent schoolgirls. They were both aware of Angela's unquenchable curiosity. Gossip was her favorite hobby; she thrived on it, and now that Jessica thought about it, she really wasn't surprised that she had heard about Stephen and her. Angela could find out anything.

Walking on North Michigan Avenue, on a stretch of road that was known as the Magnificent Mile, they passed some of the finest and most expensive shops in the world. Tiffany, Gucci, Cartier, I. Magnin, Elizabeth Arden. The street was lined with the fashion centers of the wealthy and chic.

On the left side of the street was the old water tower,

one of the few monuments left standing after the Great Chicago Fire.

For twenty-seven hours in October of 1871 most of what had been created in the city's first fifty years was reduced to ashes. Everyone blamed the fire on Mrs. O'Leary and the cow that kicked over a lantern. But regardless of what caused the blaze before the fire was checked by gun powder and rain, over eighteen thousand buildings were destroyed and ninety thousand people left homeless. Miraculously enough, only three hundred people died in the fire.

Across the street from the original water tower was a large hotel, condominium, and shopping complex known as Water Tower Place. The latter was where Angela wanted to do her shopping, so they found a restaurant that wasn't too crowded and, removing their coats, sat down in a booth in the corner.

Jessica had evaded Angela's questions thus far, but she knew the inquisition was not over.

"Look"—Angela leaned toward Jessica, her eyes squinting with itching curiosity—"are you going to deny that there is something going on between you and Stephen Dalheurst?"

"You are incurable!" Jessica laughed. "I went to a party the other night and he was there. That's it."

"That's it!" Angela was noticeably disappointed.

"That's it. Really."

"Well, what about Saint Patty's Day? I heard it through the grapevine that you were with him that night."

"You missed your calling, Angela. You should have been a spy. The CIA maybe?" They laughed before Jessica continued. "I wasn't with him," she explained patiently. "He sort of—abducted me from my date."

"Abducted you? How utterly exciting! Jessica, do you know what that does to my prurient interests?"

Jessica could well imagine, but Angela seemed intent on verbalizing precisely what it did.

"A man like Stephen Dalheurst." She was looking off into space, her eyes clouded with undisguised lust. "Just thinking about a man like him makes me all—well, you know."

Jessica blushed a crimson-red. She was shocked, even after all these years, by Angela's lack of inhibitions, and at the same time she was blushing because of her own reaction to Stephen's sex appeal.

"Really, Angela." Jessica tried to sound disgusted. "The man was practically like a brother to me. I grew up next door to him."

"Lucky you," Angela smiled. "What was he like as a little boy?"

"Well, actually, he was never little in my eyes. He was my brother's age—eight years older than I. So he was always 'the older man.' But, to answer your question, he was really nice—more than nice. He was special." Jessica's own eyes were staring off into space, thinking of her youth and of the young Stephen Dalheurst. She smiled inwardly as she talked. "Whenever I would beg Thomas and Stephen to let me play with them or join their clubs, Stephen was always the one to convince Thomas to let me. He treated me as if I was *his* little sister."

"How romantic," Angela crooned. "I can just see the headlines—Two Childhood Sweethearts Reunited After All These Years."

"Don't you think you're being just a little bit overly dramatic?" Jessica scolded.

"Jessica, how can you not be attracted to a man like

that? I know you've always been a little uptight about—shall we say the more basic side of our natures. But really, if you don't swoon at the sight of him, then you're crazier than I thought."

"Angela, you know what Stephen is like. I know *you* read the gossip columns. He's the Valentino of the jet set."

"But that makes him that much more exciting!" Angela cried, her face filled with exasperation at Jessica's puritanical attitude.

"Not to me, Angela. Not to me."

CHAPTER SIX

By Friday night Jessica was exhausted from the feverish bustle of the past work week and the continuous sleepless nights. She would lie awake for long hours, wanting something that she wasn't able to explain.

Her life had become a riddle that she couldn't solve. She wanted Stephen, and the physical longing was so intense she would have to bury her face in the pillow to keep from screaming. But it was more than that. She despised his way of life and the way he had treated her seven years ago. Yet, at the same time, she wanted nothing more than to be with him, to love him.

On Saturday she dragged around the house, counting the hours until the weekend was over and she could drown her loneliness in work again. At night she lay in bed listening to the rhythmic ticking of the clock until she drifted off into a fitful dream-filled sleep.

The dreams had finally stopped around five o'clock in

the morning, and she had just entered a deep-sleep cycle when a loud knocking at the door startled her awake.

Trying to shake the heavy sleep from her body, she dragged herself out of bed and stumbled to her closet where she found an old blue quilted robe. She heard the impatient knock again and quickly knotted the robe sash at her waist while she walked through the living room.

Opening the door, she found herself staring into the insolent face of Stephen Dalheurst.

"What—what are you doing here? What time is it?" Her voice was groggy and gruff, but her hand had automatically raised to her head, smoothing her hair into place.

He had told her he would be in Europe for two weeks, but she didn't ask him why he was home a week early. She wasn't about to give him the satisfaction of thinking that she cared.

"It's early. I didn't want to have to compete with the Sunday drivers." Stephen had stepped into the house and was scanning the living room with his eyes, appraising every inch of it.

Shocked at his nerve—waking her up on a Sunday morning and just marching uninvited into her house—and embarrassed at not having her clothes and makeup on, Jessica challenged his presence with justifiable anger.

"I'll ask you again before you leave. What are you doing here?" He was ignoring her question, moving through the house with single-minded possessiveness, opening doors and cabinets, looking in every room. "That is, if you're through dissecting my house," she growled toward the bedroom.

Stephen reentered the living room and stopped to look at Jessica. His coat was thrown over one arm, and his other hand was in the pocket of his tan corduroy slacks. The top two buttons of his green striped shirt were open, revealing a tan, totally masculine chest beneath. His gold-flecked hair was attractively tousled, attesting to the fact that Chicago's nickname, "the windy city," was well founded. The obvious virility of the man standing before her sent shivers down Jessica's spine. The only thing that kept her from throwing herself against that masculine frame was the sardonic glint of amusement in his eyes. This was another one of his practical jokes, no doubt.

He was staring at her rumpled hair, bare face and robe-clad figure, his gaze mentally untying the robe, touching the warm, sleep-laden body, pulling her against his own hard frame. When his seductive stare was met by Jessica's icy glare, the detached amusement returned.

"Why don't you get dressed and put on some makeup. We'll talk after we're on our way." The fact that Stephen obviously had her plans all mapped out for her threw Jessica into a speechless rage.

"Who do you think you are?" she retorted when her anger finally found voice. "And what do you mean, 'after we're on our way'? You can't just walk in here and—"

Stephen had moved in front of her, his face only inches from hers. The eyes were no longer amused. They were hard and commanding. He grasped her upper arm with his hand, squeezing his fingers into her flesh. His voice was low and exacting. "I said get dressed, Jessica. You have a choice. You can either do it yourself, or I'll do it for you." That last threat triggered her body into action. Within a second she was in the bedroom, climbing into a pair of rust wool slacks and pulling on an angora turtle-neck sweater with black-and-rust stripes. It wasn't until she was in the bathroom with the door closed and her makeup drawer open that she dared stop and take a breath.

A few minutes later they were in his brown Jaguar—a chocolate-brown that matched the color of his eyes. They were driving north on Lake Shore Drive before she dared ask a question. His cold set features had prevented her from doing so before now.

"Do you mind if I ask where we're going?" It made her angry to hear her own timid voice.

"North." His eyes were staring straight ahead, his hands deftly controlling the car as it curved along the edge of the lake.

"North," she repeated, mimicking the intonation of his voice. "How far north? Evanston? Canada? The North Pole?" Her voice had regained a certain amount of flippancy.

"Cut the sarcasm, would you, Jessica?" Stephen glanced wearily at her. "I don't want to have to battle you all day, okay?" His placating tone startled her into silence. She didn't want to battle him either. Maybe she should just sit back and enjoy the Sunday drive. Did it really matter where they were going?

It was cold today, with the temperature hovering in the teens. But the sky was cloudless and bright, the sunlight casting a radiant sheen across the water of the lake. Lake Shore Drive extended from as far south as Jackson Park, winding along the lake's edge through downtown Chicago, past Lincoln Park, and on north almost to Evanston. North of downtown to Lincoln Park lay the area known as the Gold Coast. Along this stretch, the drive was massed with high-rise condominiums and luxury apartments.

After 1794, when Anthony Wayr~ beat the Indians in

the Battle of Fallen Timbers and six miles at the mouth of the Chicago River fell to the United States, a prosperous lakeport grew. Chicago began as a crossroad between lake and river traffic. Later, with the opening of the Saint Lawrence Seaway, the city evolved from a lakeport to a seaport.

Lake Michigan was the city's reason for being. Chicago boasted very little else in the way of nature's grandeur. There were no majestic mountains or balmy seacoasts; no weathered, stone canyons or gorges carved out of time; no sun-stained deserts. The lake was it. It provided the city with its drinking water, became the recreation spot for its people, acted as a powerful and sometimes sinister reflection of the weather, and determined in part the caste system of the city. With the establishment of the Gold Coast and the mansions north of the city along the lake, one's station in society was decided by how close one lived to the lake and how good one's view of it was.

The heater was on in Stephen's car, and Jessica felt warm and secure as she gazed out the window at the passing scenery.

"Do you sleep with Bill?" The question startled her out of her warm reverie. She bolted upright in the seat, turning a vindictive face toward him. He stared straight ahead, his eyes boring into the concrete in front of the car.

"What?" She jumped at his question, fiercely angry at his crude intrusions into her privacy.

"That's another way of saying, Does he make love to you." His voice carried a hint of impatience.

"I know what it means, thank you," she snapped. "And I hardly think it's any of your business."

"Oh, it's my business all right." His eyes, as they turned

toward her, were filled with a challenging possessiveness. "But I already know the answer anyway," he shrugged.

"Oh?" she retorted defiantly. "And would you like to tell me?" Though neither had wanted their conversation to turn into an argument, it was becoming just that. But Jessica certainly wasn't going to be the one to back down. She tilted her chin high as she glared at Stephen's profile.

"You don't—sleep with him, that is."

"And what makes you so sure?" God, but he was smug! Who did he think he was, analyzing her sex life this way?

"I told you. I saw the way you danced with him the other night. There was no intimacy there."

"Then why did you ask?" Her teeth were clenched together in righteous anger.

"I just wanted to hear you say it." The imperious voice had melted into a soft seriousness. They had reached the campus of Northwestern University, and Stephen eased the car into a small park by the lake. He switched off the engine and turned toward Jessica, placing his arm on the back of the seat just inches from her shoulder. He leaned his face toward her slightly.

"You have built a gilded cage around yourself so nobody can get near you, haven't you?" He paused, waiting for her to answer. When she didn't, he spoke again, his eyes burning intensely into her face. "How long has it been, Jessica?" His voice was soft and probing, but its effect on Jessica left her stinging with bitterness and exhaustion.

"How long has what been?" she asked wearily, knowing full well what he was asking.

"How long has it been since you've made love with a man? How long since you've touched and been touched?" He was speaking as if to a child.

"Well, as best as I can recall," she scathed, her lip curling with scorn, "it was a couple of weeks ago when you practically raped me in your car."

"Raped!" Stephen laughed. "Is that what you call it? Believe me, Jessie, I don't have to resort to rape to fulfill my needs. There are plenty of women out there who are more than willing to—"

"Then why don't you go get one of them?" She flung the bitter words at him. "Why do you have to bother me when I don't want you?" She was lying about not wanting him, but she would never admit to him that his touch filled her with a desire she could barely control.

"As I recall, you were enjoying my mouth and my touch as much as I was enjoying yours." His fingertips were lightly stroking her shoulder, sending electric vibrations flowing through her body.

"Stop it!" She moved away from his touch. "I want you to take me home, Stephen. I don't know what kind of cruel, sadistic game you're playing, but I want no part of it." She was angry and bitter and could no longer hide her desire to get away from him. She noticed that suddenly his eyes had clouded over, unreadable and unfathomable to her.

"No," he commanded, his voice low and hard. He immediately turned back to the wheel, started the engine, and backed out of the park onto Sheridan Road, still heading north.

"Stephen, I'm demanding that you take me home." She was desperately trying to keep the hysteria out of her voice. Stephen glanced sharply at her, his face frozen in an iron mask of grim determination, and she had to admit that, at that moment, she was afraid of him. He wasn't the same Stephen she had known seven years ago. She wasn't sure what he was capable of doing, and the thought frightened her.

"What are you trying to prove?" she asked in a slightly fearful tone.

"Have you really not figured out where I'm taking you? You really can't guess?" he hissed.

"To Benchcrest?" Her voice was barely above a whisper. The look on his face said that she had guessed right. She should have known! He was taking her to Benchcrest. Did she, somewhere in her subconscious, know all along that he was taking her there? She certainly wasn't stupid. Yes, she had known. Why had she not stopped him before they came this far? Was her desire to see her home again stronger than her desire to stay away from it? She sat huddled in the corner, sullen and quiet, licking her wounds. Her face was a collage of the strange tumultous emotions coursing through her mind.

Whereas the snow had melted in town, here up North it was still fairly deep and trackless. It was no longer soft and fluffy, but had solidified and crusted from the continuous days and nights of extreme cold. They passed through the suburban towns of Winnetka and Wilmette, their quaint shops and palatial mansions causing Jessica to shudder with unexpected excitement.

She was going home! What would it look like? Would it appear as stately and lovely as always? Her stomach was beginning to fill with butterflies, and she was surprised at her own sense of anticipation. She and Stephen had not said anything to each other since she realized where they were going. She wanted the silence and she supposed he did too.

As they continued north the lots became increasingly wooded, and the land more hilly. Ravines cut their way

95

through the thick stands of trees, flowing cold and clean through forested yards. As the road climbed higher so did the houses. Perched atop hills, many were accessible to the road below only by steep rock stairs. Jessica watched out the window as a solitary bird circled above the thicket of trees, alone in its search for warmth and foliage in which to make its home.

As they approached the private road leading to Benchcrest, Jessica's excitement was almost uncontrollable. She held her hands tightly clenched in her lap and breathed deeply to control the bubbling inside her stomach. She could not read his expression—or his mind—to know why Stephen was taking her home. But right now she didn't care. She was going home!

They turned right onto the gravel road, the snow, as always, neatly plowed to the sides. The familiarity of the curves in the road, the closely planted elms lining its edges, the occasional glimpses of the house between the trees, all crowded into her brain, producing a longing so intense she felt as if she might explode. Without thinking, she reached for Stephen, clasping his upper thigh tightly with her trembling hand. His own hand closed over hers, enveloping her homecoming in the warmth and security of his nearness.

They rounded the final curve, leaving the trees behind them to enter a large clearing where the house stood. There it was before her, as magnificent and beautiful as it had always been.

Stephen stopped the car by the front colonnade and turned off the engine. Jessica knew he was watching her, waiting for her reaction. But her mouth would not move; her surging emotions were so profound that she could only stare at the house that was her home.

Stephen stepped out of the car and walked around to her side. He opened her door and, holding her hand, lifted her out of the car. Her legs were weak with excitement and pent-up emotion, and she leaned into him as they walked up the front steps, needing his strength and support beside her. Stephen rang the doorbell, and Jessica began to shudder.

When the door opened, Jessica was looking into the shocked face of Rosita. Her surprise immediately turned to unsuppressed happiness as she wrapped her large, fleshy body around Jessica.

"Jessica! *¡Chiquita mía!*" Never taking her arms from around Jessica, Rosita turned her head into the house, yelling, *"¡Hernando! ¡Hernando! ¡Ven acá! ¡Jessica está aquí!"* Hernando came running into the room, waving his arms and grabbing Jessica away from Rosita. He gave her a tremendous bear hug, then, embarrassed by the overwhelming emotion he had displayed, he stepped back. He held his hands formally clasped in front of him and, bending at the waist slightly, said, *"Bienvenida, señorita."*

Hernando had aged considerably since Jessica had last seen him, and she could see the sixty years etched into his face. His frame was thin and slightly stooped, and his shining black hair was now streaked with gray.

Rosita, on the other hand, hardly looked a day older. Her brown skin was still smooth and supple, her cheeks plump and brown. The only sign of age on her was that her hair, too, was now sprinkled with ash-gray.

After the joyful reunion tapered off to a more subdued glow, Jessica allowed herself to be dragged through the house by Rosita and Hernando, with Stephen in tow. Rosita, never pausing for a breath, pointed out all of the repairs that had been made, describing in detail any changes in the rooms. Her round face beamed with pride as she showed Jessica each room. And she should be proud, thought Jessica. It is her house as much as mine, and for the last six years, she and Hernando have been solely responsible for its upkeep.

As though a piñata had been opened, the memories evoked by the smells and the sounds of this house flew at Jessica from all directions, leaving her breathless with their beautiful ache. She had thought that, if she came back, she would be confronted only by the emptiness, the pain, and the sadness of her family's death. She had pictured their shadows everywhere; imagined their voices invading every molecule of air. But the memories she met now were happy ones. In each room were remembrances of her childhood, of blissful moments of her youth.

They had reached the landing where a second set of stairs led into the west wing of the house, the wing where her parents' suite was. Rosita had paused and was looking nervously from Hernando to Stephen and back to Hernando again.

"Jessica?" Rosita's voice was unsure.

"I want to see my parents' room, Rosita." She wasn't sure she meant what she was saying, but seeing Rosita's skeptical look, she added a decisive tone to her words. "I really do."

Rosita again looked at Stephen for direction, and turned to walk up the stairs only after he nodded his head in approval.

As the door was opened Jessica was assaulted by a sweet, suffocating scent of untouched years. The rooms were cleaned regularly with the rest of the house, but to Jessica, the air held a sacred quality that no amount of disinfectant could erase. Here was the room where her mother and father had talked and dreamed and loved privately—and together. There was the bed she used to crawl into in the middle of the night when she was scared of the shadows in her own room.

She walked to the window overlooking the backyard and stared down at the snowy ground. How many times, when she had insisted on being a tomboy and playing rough-and-tumble games with the boys, had she looked up and seen her mother's indulgent but slightly disapproving frown?

She was staring out the window and did not see Stephen motion Rosita and Hernando out of the room, nor did she hear the door quietly closing. But she felt his hands resting gently on her shoulders and turned around to smile at him.

"Thank you," she said, unable to express how deeply she was affected by his thoughtfulness.

"Your welcome."

She turned back to look out the window, and his arms circled her from behind. She leaned into his body, her head resting against his chest. Certain painful memories about her family were beginning to surface, but in his arms she felt safe from them.

"Just because you're born privileged doesn't mean you're always privileged, does it?" She was in a pensive mood, but she wanted to share her thoughts—to share them with Stephen.

"No . . . no, it doesn't." He kissed her temple lightly. "But at least you're not alone. Everybody suffers . . . in one way or another."

How have you suffered, Stephen? she wondered. Another time or place, she might have felt bitterness toward him for his remark. But now she heard only sincerity in his voice, and she clung to the tenderness of the moment.

"Did you think I was a tomboy?" she asked suddenly, returning to her thoughts of a few moments earlier.

"Yes."

"Yes!" She was a little shocked by his blunt honesty and a little hurt too. Maybe, because of her former tomboyishness, she didn't hold the right kind of appeal for him. But then she saw his smile, a playful curve of his lips that reminded her of the Stephen she once knew. "You're terrible!" She pouted at him.

"Well, you asked. Besides"—he murmured through lips that trailed past her ear to kiss the sensitive skin of her neck—"what's wrong with being healthy and outdoorsy?"

"I always preferred indoor activity myself," she purred seductively.

"Now who's being a tease?" He gently bit the lobe of her ear before turning her to face him. His eyes were soft and tender, and she had no misgivings about slipping her arms around his waist and letting him hold her close to his body.

But, realizing where she was, she felt a sudden surge of emotion, the ghostly memories she had been expecting finally penetrating her dazed mind.

Reluctant as she was to leave the circle of his arms, she pushed away. Looking distractedly at the furnishings in the room, she felt tears stinging the backs of her eyes.

"I—I can't stay in here." She was walking quickly to the bedroom door.

"Jessica—wait." Stephen tried to call her back, but she had already run down the stairs and was clinging to the banister for emotional support.

"The room . . . the memories . . ." She couldn't begin to explain her feelings.

"I know." He took her elbow, loosening her grip on the banister. "Let's go downstairs. I'll bet Rosita will fix us something to drink."

She smiled weakly and let him lead her down the stairs to the kitchen. Rosita and Hernando were there, seated at the big round table.

The warm wood-scented kitchen, the oak-lined cabinets and brown brick floor, were a gentle foil for the bright yellow pattern in the curtains and tablecloth. They sat around the table while Rosita fixed hot chocolate, and the conversation turned to lighter topics, dulling the pain Jessica had been feeling a few moments earlier. Rosita was full of chatter about what they had been doing, kidding Hernando about his graying hair.

"So, Jessica, what do you think?" she asked, putting a pan of milk on the stove.

"Well, I don't know. Everything seems so small!" With Rosita's running commentary, Jessica had not been able to say much of anything. Her words now came out in a breathless flow.

"Small!" exclaimed Rosita, her eyes wide and her mouth hanging open. "*¡Diós mío!* Do you hear this girl, Hernando?" Leaning down close to Jessica, her eyes crinkling at the edges, she said "You must live in very big house now. No?"

"No," Jessica quickly corrected. "It's not that the house seems small, it's just that—I don't know. Everything in it seems so little compared to the way I remember it. That dish drain, for instance." She pointed to the counter where the dishes were drying. "It's strange, but it seems so little. And that window over the sink. It seems so low."

After what seemed to Jessica like a long silence, Stephen began laughing softly, as if indulging the bewilderment of a child. "You've been away for a long time, Jessie. You were a child when you left here. It's only natural that everything should seem so small to you."

"But I was almost twenty," she argued, not yet comprehending his point.

"Your brain has grown," explained Rosita, now understanding. "You no longer see the world as a child. ¿Es verdad, Señor Stephen?"

"That's right. It puts new perspective on the way you see things that seemed so large as a child," Stephen added. Jessica wondered if he had a double meaning in mind when he said this. Perhaps he was warning her that her memories of him were larger in her mind than they were in actuality; maybe that was the reason for bringing her here.

She had no time to reflect on this, because Rosita set the cups of steaming hot chocolate on the table and turned to Stephen. "So what you think of new paint in bedroom, Señor Stephen?"

"I like it. It looks very nice," he replied, avoiding Jessica's curious look.

"That man you sent to do the job"—Rosita continued, handing each person a paper napkin—"he work very fast, but very careful not to make mess."

"Man *you* sent?" Jessica was staring at Stephen, a look of surprise in her eyes.

Before he could answer, Rosita did. "Oh, *sí*. Señor Stephen help out so much around here. You are lucky to have such a kind friend."

"It's really nothing," he shrugged his shoulders, his eyes meeting Jessica's with a look of appeasement. "I just

102

drop by every so often when I'm in town . . . to make sure everything's okay. Actually," he added, laughing nervously, "it's to get one of Rosita's home-cooked meals." Realizing he had not answered Jessica's question, he continued. "This painter I know owed me a favor, so I sent him over to put on a fresh coat of paint in the room. It was no big deal."

Jessica said nothing, but she watched his expression intently, trying to make sense of this new revelation. Her own expression reflected a mixture of curiosity and reproach that Stephen would have the nerve to decide which rooms in *her* house needed paint. However, she would not confront him on the issue now. She would wait until they were away from Rosita and Hernando.

"When are you moving back in, *chiquita*? The house, it is so empty without your mama and papa and Tomás, God rest their souls." Rosita crossed herself with her right hand, and her eyes clouded with a weathered sadness.

At the mention of her family a lump formed in Jessica's throat. She had known the topic would come up sooner or later, but she wasn't ready to talk about it yet. She took a big gulp of the hot liquid, its heat burning a path down her throat. She stood up quickly and began slipping on her coat.

"I think I'll look at the grounds." She kept her face averted from theirs so that they would not see the tears that were beginning to form.

Hernando stood up quickly and reached for his own coat, which was on the hook by the back door. "Of course, señorita, I will show you around." Jessica knew he was eager to please and comfort her, for she hadn't fooled any of them. But what she wanted right now was to be alone.

"No, thank you, Hernando. I'd like to just walk around

103

on my own." She was fighting now to keep the tears back. She hurriedly opened the back door and rushed out into the chill air, closing the door swiftly behind her.

The cold air froze the tears as they dropped from her eyes; she was unable to control them now. She let them come, silent heaving sobs racking her upper body, washing away the years of grief and loneliness. She did not hear the back door open, but she felt herself wrapped in the warmth of someone's strong arms—Stephen's arms—holding her as she cried the tears that had been waiting so long to come. She let Stephen hold her head against his chest, needing once again his strength and tenderness. His head bent down and his lips brushed softly across the top of her head, his hand gently stroking the back of her hair.

She cried until the tears were spent. Slowly she raised her head from his chest and wiped her face with the back of her hand. Stephen pulled a handkerchief from his pocket and wiped the tears from her face. She smiled weakly at him and was rewarded with a soft expression of tenderness. His eyes were soft and kind, the liquid brown pools washing over her face with affection. Like those that had looked upon her with tenderness in her parents' bedroom, these were the eyes she remembered, the Stephen she had clung to for the last seven years. He slipped his arm around her shoulder, and they began walking through the grounds of Benchcrest.

Though the air was bitingly cold, Jessica once again felt warm and secure in the circle of Stephen's arm. They seemed an integral part of the natural order of life at Benchcrest.

CHAPTER SEVEN

Only an acre of the grounds around the estate was tended. The rest was left natural and wild, existing as nature had intended. The upper grounds were manicured and contained. Large beds of spirea, forsythia, and rose of Sharon dominated the landscape closest to the house, their branches bleak and naked in the dead of winter. But when spring came, their blossoms would fill the air with color and a sweet, delicate fragrance.

The sun had moved farther west in the sky, casting long frigid shadows over much of the yard, their cold, lifeless shapes tightly hugging the ground. But Jessica, her body surrounded by the warmth of Stephen's arm, didn't seem to notice the cold.

In the south corner of the lawn lay the tennis courts and now empty swimming pool with cabana. Jessica loved to play tennis and had kept up with the sport since leaving Benchcrest. She spent several evenings a month at the tennis club downtown, perfecting her already well-honed game.

Instead of walking toward the pool and courts, they headed north into the wooded thicket between Stephen's childhood home and hers. The snow was deep and crackling under their feet, and she was glad she had worn her heavily lined boots. Snow-covered mounds of buried leaves added variety to the solid sheet of white. A few of the trees still clung tenaciously to their leaves, holding fast to the thread of life.

"Look over there." Jessica pointed to a grouping of trees whose branches bent low to the ground, forming a natural enclosure.

Stephen looked in the direction she was pointing and Jessica watched the smile that played upon his lips. They walked over to the bower, pushing the stiff branches aside to enter. The inside diameter was about nine feet, large enough for children to play in, but small enough to retain a cozy atmosphere.

"Remember how we used to hold club meetings in here?" Jessica was enjoying the childhood memory.

"Yes." Stephen's voice was slightly wistful. "But it seems like Thomas used to change the rules for club membership every other day."

"Well, but you always had to be president, remember?" She nudged him with her elbow, teasing him with the reminder.

His look was one of sheepish resignation. "That's true." He shrugged.

"You were a tyrant, even then." She laughed, but her eyes held a twinge of defiance.

"What do you mean, 'Even then'?" He looked at her

with his chin tilted high, daring her to back up her accusation with an example.

She was enjoying their easy relationship too much to upset the newly established equilibrium. "I was just teasing," she defended.

Standing in the natural protection of the shelter, she saw that Stephen's eyes were moving seductively over her coat-covered body, mentally peeling the layers of clothes from her frame. The blaze from his eyes warmed her body to the bone and she had forcefully to tear her gaze from his before she became lost in their smoldering depths.

She quickly pushed aside the branches and stepped out into the open woods. She breathed deeply, hoping the chill air would still the rapid pounding of her heart. It would be so easy to fall into his arms, to wrap their bodies around each other and find warmth in each other's touch.

She surmised that her reaction to him was due to both the intense emotional experience of coming home for the first time in six years and his tender strength and comfort, which she had been able to rely on when she broke down in tears a few minutes earlier. But, she mustn't let the desires of her body trap her into a situation that she was not ready to handle.

She stuffed her hands in the pockets of her coat and began walking east, out of the woods and toward the lake. Stephen quickly caught up with her, fully aware, she was sure, of the physical and emotional barrier she was putting between them.

She was walking instinctively east without thinking. When she realized where she was heading, she stopped in her tracks and turned back toward the house. But before she could take a step, Stephen grabbed her arm, turning her back toward the lake.

"Where do you think you're going?" The look of authority had returned.

"I—I want to go back now." She tried to avoid his penetrating eyes. "I'm cold," she lied. She wasn't cold. The heat from Stephen's nearness kept all chill from her body. But that was the only excuse she could think of. She couldn't tell him that she didn't want to face the spot on the cliff where they had first made love; where she had given herself, body and soul, to him. Forever. She could not face the memory of all that she had lost.

But his fingers were gripping her arm tightly, pulling her toward the lake. There was no angry demand in the pressure of his fingers this time, but the powerful intention was there just the same.

The trees spread apart, allowing a wide view of the lake. It was the color of liquid sapphire. Jessica leaned over the edge of the steep cliff and watched as frigid water lapped at the icy crust that clung to the ragged rocks below.

From this vantage point the lake—at every season—was beautiful and dazzling in its endless variety. Enveloping herself in the surroundings, she turned to look at the house, perched majestically and proudly on the terraced lawn. God, but it was beautiful.

"Beautiful, isn't it?" said Stephen, echoing her own thoughts.

The sights and the smells were so breathtakingly beautiful that Jessica could only nod.

Jessica turned back to the lake, and Stephen turned with her. He was looking out across the water, but his words were directed to her. "You belong here, Jessica." She thought that his voice had trembled slightly with the statement. And, though she wanted to believe that she belonged here, she could not. It was a beautiful fantasy, but it had nothing to do with reality.

"You can't go home again, haven't you heard?" Jessica's voice was distant and flat, a hint of bitterness underlying her tone.

"That depends," said Stephen, looking down at the snow, pondering something more significant than white-carpeted ground.

Her head jerked up to look at him, a wariness automatically tightening the muscles of her face. "On what?" she cautiously asked.

"On how you approach it." He had turned his head to look at her, his eyes searching her expression for the hidden secrets it held. His face revealed a new expression, a new softness that Jessica had not seen since they were young. She sensed that he was groping for the appropriate words before he spoke again. "If you expect to return as a child, then you're right. You can't go back; too many things have changed for that." He looked again at the shimmering sapphire water, but not before Jessica had detected the sharp pain that shadowed his face. "Too many dreams have been lost."

He was silent for a long moment. Jessica had never seen Stephen at a loss for words before, and she wondered if she should say something—anything. When he turned toward her, his eyes were dark and intense. She sensed that he had more to say, and she was relieved, for she did not trust her own voice to speak. "But if you choose to come back as a woman and"—he strained again for the right word— "open yourself to the past in a new—as a woman. . . ." He let the thought trail off, forcing her to extract the elusive meaning in his words.

Though her hands wanted to reach out and touch his arm, to comfort and find comfort in the warmth of his strong, muscular body, she kept them imprisoned in the pockets of her coat.

How could she tell him that she could not move back to Benchcrest? That she could not constantly face the lonely ache she felt for him? She had always thought that she stayed away from Benchcrest because of the memories of her family. But, she now had to admit, it was more than that.

Stephen was the primary reason. She could not deal with the torturous memories of him. For he was a part of Benchcrest as much as she was. She would hear his voice, no more than a whisper, still echoing through the dense woods. Every time she touched the rich brown soil, she would be reminded of the color of his eyes. And she would smell his distinctive male scent lingering in the air. No. She would never escape his memory if she moved back here. The only way to forget him was to bury herself in the city, in her job, and in the cold dark tomb of passionless existence.

"I can't Stephen." Her voice was filled with pain as she turned toward the house. "We had better get back now. Rosita and Hernando will be wondering where we are."

"To hell with Rosita and Hernando." His voice was husky and low. "I've got a better idea."

Wrapping his arms around her waist, he pulled her against his body.

"You won't change my mind," she declared, her eyes steady with determination.

"We'll see," he replied softly.

His brown eyes never left her face as his hands moved down to her hips and held them tightly against his length, making her fully aware of the idea he had in mind. The feel of their bodies so close, her hips pressed against him, left her weak with desire. Her eyes were glued to his face, watching the smoldering eyes that were watching her, the mouth that was descending upon hers. When their lips met, she felt the overpowering electric ache in her loins. She wanted to be consumed by it. She wanted to lie on the snowy bed between the trees. She wanted to feel Stephen's hard body upon hers. She wanted to satisfy the burning ache inside her. She wanted nothing more than to make love to him on this spot, where she had made love to him seven years ago. But she did not want to lose him. If she gave in to him now, would the next seven years of her life be a repeat of the last seven? She wanted to believe that this time things would be different. She wanted to believe it, but she could not. Was this his reason for bringing her here? Was his whole purpose to seduce her in the same spot where he had done so before? She couldn't believe that he would be that coldly deliberate, but she also couldn't take the chance.

"Stephen," she whispered, pulling reluctantly away from him. "I've had—there've been lots of memories here today that I've had to face for the first time . . . in a long time. Please try to understand. I mean, I know you think I'm a tease—"

"Jessica, I was just frustrated when I said that before. I didn't really mean it." His voice sounded genuinely apologetic.

"Well, maybe you're right. Maybe I have been making you think that I—this is very difficult for me to say, but—" She sighed heavily. "I want to go home now and I—I don't think we should see each other again." She was looking out across the water, avoiding his face. She knew

111

that if she had looked into his eyes, she would never have been able to say that, never been able to put an end to something she wanted more than anything in the world.

She braced herself for the onslaught of derisive remarks that she knew would be forthcoming. When they didn't come, she was surprised. She was even more surprised when he took her gently by the elbow and led her through the trees and up the lawn to the house. She chanced a look at his profile and was confused by the expression there. There was no anger, no impatience. His eyes and mouth held, instead, a look of unflinching determination, as if he had come to a decision of his own. He said nothing; the empty silence became almost unbearable to her. She would have almost preferred his abusive verbal assault to this oppressive, deafening quiet.

By the time they reached the house, she couldn't wait to break away from him and his silence and find solace in Rosita's nonstop chatter. She was relieved to find Rosita and Hernando still waiting for them in the kitchen. She dreaded the long drive back with Stephen but, at the same time, wanted to get it over with, so she declined an offer of more hot chocolate. It was Hernando who brought up the subject of her future.

"Did you decide, señorita?" His voice was shy and respectful. "Are you coming back to Benchcrest to stay?"

"Hernando. Rosita." Jessica began, choosing her words very carefully. "I'm afraid that's imposs—"

"As a matter of fact," Stephen interrupted, his tone brusque and decisive, "she will be moving her things back in this week. Tomorrow."

"Stephen!" Jessica's cry fell on deaf ears.

"Señorita!" Rosita exclaimed. "That's wonderful. Hernando do you hear this? She is coming home. We are so happy!"

"No! Wait a minute." Jessica was panicked. "There's a mistake. Stephen, tell them, for God's sake!"

"Jessica's right. I should tell you. She doesn't want you to go to any trouble. Don't plan anything special. She wants to just quietly move back in with no fanfare." Her mouth was gaping at Stephen with disbelief, but the look he gave her indicated that she had better keep her mouth shut. It was a hard look, a powerful look, and she wasn't sure she wanted to find out what would happen if she disobeyed. When he was sure she had understood his silent message, he took her arm and led her toward the front door. "Come on, Jessica. We've got to get back now. Remember, Rosita," he called back over his shoulder. "Nothing special. We'll just move the things quietly back in tomorrow evening."

"*Sí, señor*. Nothing special. We will be waiting for you. *Adiós*."

"Good-bye," Stephen said for both of them. Jessica was in too much shock to speak, but she raised her hand in farewell.

She waited until the car was pulling out of the drive and heading down the gravel driveway leading to the main road before she spoke. "What on earth did you do that for? Why would you tell them something like that? I don't understand you at all, Stephen. How could you lie to them that way?"

"Lie? I didn't lie to them." His face had retained the determined expression. "I meant every word I said."

"I told you . . . only fifteen minutes ago . . . that I was not moving back in. I meant every word I said too."

The car turned onto Sheridan Road, heading south toward Chicago. The afternoon sun was covered by gray clouds, bringing more chill to the air. Stephen drove a half a mile before he decided to speak. Before he did, he pulled the car onto a side road, pulling to the curb and shifting the car into park. He left the car running so the heater would continue to fill the car with its warmth. He turned in his seat to face Jessica. His eyes showed signs of weariness, but the tireless determination was still evident.

"Tomorrow you're going to tell Caldwell that you're quitting your job—or taking a leave of absence, if you'd rather." He did not pause as the look of incredulity spread across Jessica's face. "Tomorrow night we are going to move your personal things into Benchcrest. We'll leave the furniture. Your town house will be a good place to spend the night if we're ever in the city for a late evening. Tuesday morning," he continued, "we'll move my things into Benchcrest. Wednesday morning we'll have a justice of the peace marry us and then we'll hop on a plane for London where I have a very important business meeting to go to on Thursday. After the meeting we'll have two weeks in Europe for our honeymoon. Then we'll come back to Benchcrest to live. Any questions?"

Jessica was stunned. She could not move, or speak, or breathe. Married! Stephen was asking her to marry him. No. He was telling her that she was going to marry him. But it didn't matter. The fact was that he wanted her to marry him! The thought reverberated through her mind, constricting the flow of all other thoughts. She didn't know how long she sat there paralyzed, staring with wide bewildered eyes at his face. She didn't even notice when the air began to recirculate through her lungs.

But she heard Stephen continue as if there had been no break in his conversation. He kept his hands firmly planted on his legs, not daring to reach out and touch her. "I hadn't really planned to ask you this way. It's not too romantic, I suppose. I'm afraid I'm not as good at romance as the journalists like to portray me. Maybe I'm just too old for games, but . . . when you said you didn't want to see me again, well, I knew I had to do something fast." His hand reached out to take hers. "I can't stand the thought of you with Bill—with anyone else. When you were in college, I used to think of you with other guys, and it would tear me to pieces." He stopped, his breath rapid and uneven. When he spoke, his voice was a painfully husky whisper. "I've had a ripping ache in my gut for so—so many years, Jessie. I can't stand it any longer. Please . . . marry me!"

The thought that he had been the one to reject her seven years ago did not stray to the surface of her conscious mind now. She was so filled with surprise and joy, she thought of nothing but the desperate, burning love she had for him. Their eyes locked in a fiery embrace.

"Yes," she whispered, barely hearing her own voice. "I'll marry you, Stephen."

Their bodies leaned toward each other, their lips colliding in a burning seal of their love. Jessica felt herself being lifted by his strong arms into his lap. With heavy winter clothes and coats on, it was crowded in the tiny confined space behind the steering wheel, but neither seemed to notice. Their mouths were clinging to each other, his tongue driving deep into her mouth. His right hand pulled at the knot holding her coat together. Once released, his hand plunged inside the coat, pushing up under her sweater and bra and grasping her throbbing breast. The touch of his fingers immediately hardened the nipple to a stiff peak, and burning flames raced through her veins.

She couldn't get enough of him; she wanted to touch him, to feel all of him against her. But the confines of the car made it impossible. They both realized this, and though neither wanted to pull away from the other's mouth, the torture of not being able to satisfy their desires was too much.

When he pulled his lips from hers, they moved to her ear. His breath was ragged and hard, and he started to speak. But, prolonging the exquisite torture a little longer, he nipped at the lobe of her ear, his tongue gliding slowly down the vein of her neck. "God, why do I have to have a sports car? Why couldn't it be a van with a bed in the back? Or even a fifty-six Chevy?"

Jessica pulled her face away, laughing at his musings of frustration. "We can wait until we're married, can't we?" Her voice sounded unsure, the nearness of him making rational thought difficult.

"Do we have to?" Stephen's hand caressed her cheek, his fingers pulling through the strands of her hair.

She didn't want to wait. She wanted to go back to the house and make passionate love for the rest of the day. But something inside her, some wariness and uncertainty, nagged at her. She could not risk giving herself to him and then losing him again. She had to wait. She would have to convince him to wait.

"It's only three days," she reminded him, hating herself for her rationality.

"Three days," he groaned. "Why didn't I say we'd get married tomorrow and move into the house on Tuesday or Wednesday?"

She smiled sympathetically at him. She knew exactly how he felt. "Don't we have to get blood tests or something?"

"Yes. I was thinking we could do that tomorrow after you talk to Caldwell. Hey, Jessica," he paused, a serious look covering his face. "Get off my lap."

"What!" she exclaimed, surprised at his brusque tone.

"If you stay here any longer, I will not claim responsibility for my actions." She laughed, noticing his grimace of frustration. She slipped back over onto her seat and Stephen put the car into drive, moving back onto the road.

"Stephen, do you want me to quit my job?" She wanted to get their conversation and thoughts on another track.

"No. I mean, not if you don't want to. But I want to let you know this. I own quite a few companies and have a considerable amount of capital from those businesses that needs to be invested, and I need someone with quite a bit of expertise—like you—to do that. I want you to handle the investments for the businesses." That statement was not issued as a request, nor was it in the tone of a demand. It was a simple statement of fact, as if God had handed Moses a new commandment.

"But, Stephen, surely you have people who do this sort of— I know nothing of your business. . . . I don't know what to say." She was thrilled that he would trust her judgment enough to request such a thing of her, but she felt totally inadequate to handle the job.

"You will know everything there is to know once you've familiarized yourself with the operations," he pointed out.

He began describing his businesses, and Jessica was astonished to learn how vast his holdings actually were. He owned boat-manufacturing firms all over the world, a substantial interest in one of Chicago's newspapers, two hotels in France and one in New York, the only American franchise for unique children's toys from the Netherlands, one-third ownership in a southwestern brewery, and sizable interests in many other smaller companies located in the United States and Europe.

His businesses required him to travel frequently all over the world; hence, the meeting in London on Thursday.

How would she ever make sense of the vast amount of holdings he had? Stephen obviously had a confidence in her ability that she herself did not have. She turned to face him with the intention of telling him that she just couldn't possibly do it, but the look in his eyes told her that he was fully aware of her intended mutiny and that there was no way she was getting out of it. Moving ahead with his decision to use her expertise, he began outlining the structure within his companies.

She listened intently to every word he said, certain of her inability to comprehend it all. She was so absorbed that she was not even aware of the scenery speeding past the car window. She listened, and soon it all began to tie together. She could see the patterns; she could understand the direction in which he wanted to go with each particular company. She listened and she asked questions every so often. She was enthralled by the operation of the various businesses; that they were Stephen's businesses made the subject even more palatable.

"You asked earlier if I didn't already have people who handled these things. The answer is yes—and no. In some instances—well, for example, with Dal-Craft Boats, I have a treasurer who handles the investments. However, he nearly always consults with me on any major transactions. I want to know what you think ahead of time, so that I can go in to him with more in mind about what I want to do. Understand?"

She nodded that she understood.

He continued. "With the hotels I've been the one to

make the investment decisions. And frankly I'm tired. I've got so much else I should be concentrating on, I need someone to handle that end of the business. I had been thinking of hiring someone, but you would be perfect for the job." As he talked she knew he wasn't looking at her as his future wife; He was looking at her as a business partner. It made her very happy to know that he could look at her with the respect in business that she had worked so hard to get.

"Of course, you know," he reminded her, "that you'll have to stay on top of the market—and the economy in general." He softened, glancing over at her with eyes full of tenderness and love. His hand reached out and brushed aside a lock of hair that had fallen across her forehead.

Talking about business had made the trip back to the city seem breathtakingly short. Stephen pulled up to her town house, easing the car into the curb. He kept his hands on the wheel and stared out the front window. "I'm not going to come in with you, Jessie, because I know if I do, I won't be able to keep my hands off you. That is, unless you've changed your mind about waiting." He looked at her with a glimmer of hope in his eyes.

"No, Stephen. I want to wait." Her determination was as strong as ever. As soon as she was his wife, she would surrender herself completely to him. But until then, she could not take the risk.

"Jessie." Though her hand was on the handle of the car door, she paused before opening it. "I guess I haven't told you that I love you, have I?"

She shook her head slowly, holding in the breath she had just taken.

"Well . . . I do." He turned his face toward her and his

eyes, though revealing little emotion, were clear and direct.

Jessica walked up the steps to her house, confident in the knowledge that she had no reason not to believe him.

CHAPTER EIGHT

The marriage ceremony was a simple one, performed by a justice of the peace, with Rosita and Hernando as witnesses to the union. Jessica and Stephen had to wait until Tuesday to take their blood tests, but by Tuesday afternoon the results were back and the marriage took place first thing Wednesday morning.

For Jessica Monday and Tuesday had passed in a confused blur. Still so astounded by the sudden turn of events in her life, she was only vaguely aware of her actions. She and Stephen moved her things into Benchcrest on Monday night, after she had informed Bob Caldwell that she would be taking a leave of absence. She knew that if she were to handle all of Stephen's investments, it would be a full-time job. Yet something held her back, something kept her from impetuously quitting her job. Surprised— but politely pleased about the impending marriage—Mr. Caldwell assured her that her job would still be waiting for her. On Tuesday morning the blood tests were taken and, while they waited for the results, they moved Stephen's things into the house.

Now, almost too quickly, the marriage ceremony was over, and they were sitting on the runway in the plane that was to take them to London. Mr. and Mrs. Dalheurst. Jessica looked once again at the first-class tickets for confirmation that this was real. It was not a dream; they were married. Her ticket plainly read MRS. STEPHEN DALHEURST.

From her seat she watched the man who was now her husband store his suit coat in the overhead storage compartment. His strong, lean body looked powerfully attractive in the dark suit pants and white dress shirt he was wearing. He had removed his coat and tie and the top button of his shirt was open, revealing the soft curling hairs on his tanned chest. She felt an involuntary shudder at the thought of tomorrow night, when she would finally have his body next to hers; when they would be able to share the love that she had waited so long to share with him.

Seeing her shudder, he sat back down in the seat beside her and patted her hand reassuringly. "You look a little nervous. You aren't afraid of flying, are you?"

"No," she assured him, not confiding what had made her shudder. It was true that she had never flown in a private aircraft since her family's crash, but her fear did not carry over to larger commercial planes.

"Good, because you will be doing a lot of flying in the next few years with me," he informed her.

She smiled and turned her head to look out the window at the long line of planes in front of theirs, waiting to take off from O'Hare Airport. She was looking at the planes, but she was thinking about her husband. There was so little she knew about the man sitting next to her. The childhood friend, the next-door neighbor she grew up with, she knew quite well, but the grown man, the adult Stephen Dalheurst, she knew nothing about. She knew little—other than what she had read—about his social life, his friends, his ex-girlfriends and lovers, his views on life in general. She knew only that she loved him. But there were so many questions still unanswered, questions she wanted, but was afraid, to ask. Why had he left her seven years ago? Why did he visit Benchcrest frequently? Why, suddenly, did he reappear in her life and take control of it? A disquieting shiver shook her body.

"A blanket for my wife, please." Jessica heard Stephen ask the stewardess for the blanket. My wife. He called her his wife. As he draped the blanket over her body she felt her heart and her entire being expand with love, a love that washed away all the questions, all the doubt. She was his wife and, for now, that was all that mattered. The time for questions would come later.

The flight from Chicago to London was a long one, eight hours and fifty minutes. For the first two hours Stephen looked through papers in his briefcase while Jessica amused herself with magazines and a book she had brought along.

The flight attendants kept the passengers so busy with champagne and meals, snacks and movies, that there was very little awareness of the passing of time.

Now the movie was over and the lights in the cabin of the plane were dimmed. The only sounds came in unobtrusive, hushed tones, an occasional cough, or a stewardess walking down the aisle. It was a dreamlike atmosphere, and Jessica had the feeling of being suspended in time and space.

Leaning back in her seat, her eyes closed, Jessica pulled the blanket over her chest. Fatigue from the last three days was catching up with her and, lulled by the monotonous hum of the plane's engines, she felt herself drifting into a semiconscious state of sleep.

The touch of a hand on her stomach woke her. She opened her eyes to see Stephen pulling her head onto his shoulder, his hand gently massaging her stomach under the blanket.

She had worn a soft beige knit dress for the simple wedding, knowing that it would be the most comfortable thing she had to wear on the long flight to England. The feel of his hand moving across the surface of her dress stirred awake the warm, restless desire within her.

"I wish we could have—"

"Spent the night in a hotel before going to London?" He finished the sentence for her. "So do I. This meeting tomorrow morning is just too important to miss, though." His breath was shallow and quick, his own body wanting the taste of satisfied desire. "If I could have, I would. Believe me."

"I know," she whispered breathlessly. "Too bad planes don't come with bedrooms."

He laughed huskily. "Tomorrow night. . . . I promise you that tomorrow night we'll make up for it."

"Hmm," she sighed, her insides seething at the promise. She readjusted the blanket to cover them both and snuggled her head closer to his neck. The softly quiet environment in the interior of the plane wrapped them in a cocoon of languid sensuousness; they were alone on an island in space, captivated by their acutely tuned senses.

Under the cover, his hand played along the expanse of her abdomen, causing the stirring embers to smolder in

124

her veins. Slowly and surreptitiously he opened the buttons of her dress and slipped his hand inside to touch the warm, inviting skin beneath. His hand closed around her breast, his thumb gently stroking the nipple to a peak.

Her breathing was quick and uneven as she turned her lips to kiss his neck. She could feel the pulse there pounding erratically and she ran her tongue along the length of the sensitive vein. At this moment she knew she wanted nothing more out of life than to be with him, to be a part of him wherever he might be.

He turned his face to kiss the top of her head and pulled her more tightly to him. His hand had slid down her bare stomach and his fingers were slipping along the thin elastic band of her panties. At the searing touch of his hand on her lower abdomen, she reached over and clasped his thigh with her own hand. She heard his sharp intake of breath and felt the hardened muscles of his thigh.

This was insane! Why were they torturing themselves so? There was no way they could satisfy the burning ache inside them, and yet the sweet pain of the moment was something that neither of them would or could put an end to—not just yet.

They arrived at London's Gatwick Airport at seven in the morning. The excitement of being in London outweighed the fatigue and jet lag that Jessica was feeling before they landed. If someone had told her a week ago that she would be coming to London as Stephen's wife, she would never have believed it. Yet, here she was in London —as Mrs. Stephen Dalheurst. There was going to be so much to see and do today that she refused to let the weariness take control of her. After brushing her hair and freshening her makeup, she met Stephen at the front door of the terminal. She had assumed they would be taking a taxi into London and was surprised to find a sleek black limousine waiting for them.

"Is that yours?" she marveled as Stephen handed her baggage to the driver.

"Well, actually I now own a half interest in it," he said, smiling, then counting the bags to make sure they had everything.

"Oh? Who's the other partner?" she asked.

"You."

"Me?" She stared curiously at Stephen as the driver held the door open for her to step in.

"Sure," he said, his voice crisp and decisive. "Everything I have is half yours."

She said nothing as she climbed into the spacious back seat of the limousine. All of her life she had been wealthy. But she had not been accustomed to riding in limousines. She was having enough trouble realizing that Stephen was really hers. It was too much to accept, or even care, that all of his wealth was hers as well.

They drove in silence most of the way into the city. Stephen was once again absorbed in his work and had strewn papers across much of the backseat. But for Jessica the forty-five minute drive into the city passed quickly. She enjoyed watching the unfamiliar scenery they passed. It was cool and overcast, and the car sliced through the thin mist clinging to the air. She leaned back in her seat, content with the moment, with the place, and with her life.

Stephen had stopped working and was now thumbing through the business section of *The Times,* London's conservative newspaper.

"Is it always cloudy like this?" Jessica asked quietly, almost afraid to interrupt his reading.

"Hmm?" He glanced up absently. "Oh, the weather?" He peeked out the car window. "No, just about ninety percent of the time." He smiled before returning to his reading.

The peaceful contentment she had felt a few moments before was beginning to disintegrate. The closer they got to London, the more Jessica's stomach began to fill with butterflies.

In a few minutes she was going to be entering Stephen's office as his wife. What would people think of her? Would she be considered a suitable choice for his wife? Probably not, she surmised with chagrin. Everyone probably expected him to marry someone famous or beautiful or someone with a slightly scandalous past of her own.

Jessica looked down disdainfully at her plain dress and felt dowdy and unattractive. Why hadn't Stephen told her she wasn't dressed properly? Didn't he care what people thought of her? Probably not, she mused, laughing to herself. She doubted if Stephen cared very much what people thought of him or of his choice in a wife. If he cared, he would have either hidden his private life from the press in the past, or else he would have fulfilled their expectations by choosing a more predictable and acceptable woman to be his wife.

Well, there wasn't much point in worrying about it now. She certainly couldn't change her looks or her rather uninteresting background; what she was would simply have to suffice.

They turned down a wide street, and Stephen pointed to a tall stone building on the left. "That's it," he said to Jessica. The driver pulled the limousine to the curb and turned off the engine. Before Jessica could grasp the door handle, the driver had opened her door and was extending a hand to help her out.

Placing her hand in the crook of Stephen's arm, she walked to the elevator, trying to conceal the nervousness she felt inside. Stephen reached over with his right hand and patted hers reassuringly. She hadn't fooled him, and she probably wouldn't fool anyone else either. Her nerves were jittery and her stomach churning as they rode silently up the elevator. The offices of Dalheurst-Pierce, Inc., occupied the entire seventh floor. The decor of the reception room was warm and welcoming and what one would expect in an old London building—brown wood tones and the strong smell of leather furniture and tobacco. A pretty receptionist smiled as they approached.

"Hello, Mr. Dalheurst," she said in a distinctly British accent. "Welcome back." She was eyeing Jessica with little curiosity. Jessica supposed that Stephen often arrived with unfamiliar women; she was probably thought to be just another one of a long line of companions.

Stephen pushed open the double wooden doors leading into the suites of offices. Greetings rang from every doorway and desk: "Hello, Stephen." "Welcome back, Mr. Dalheurst."

Jessica was wondering if he was going to introduce her as his wife when he finally stopped in the doorway to one of the private offices.

"Blane, I want you to meet—come on in here, Jessica." Jessica entered the thickly paneled office and smiled at the older man behind the desk. "This is Jessica." Stephen closed the door behind them. "Jessica, this is one of my partners, Blane Mosley." Blane stood politely behind his desk and nodded pleasantly to Jessica. "We're married," Stephen added in a soft voice.

128

"Married!" Blane half yelled, walking around from behind his desk.

"Shhh!" Stephen held a finger to his lips. "Keep it quiet, okay? I don't want all of them making a big deal." He cocked his head in the direction of the office staff beyond the door.

Why not? Jessica wondered. She wanted a big deal made of it. She was his wife and she wanted everyone to know it. Why didn't he? She had little time to speculate about his secretiveness, because Blane was walking toward her and wrapping his arms around her.

"You old son of a gun," he said to Stephen in a definitely American accent. "Jessica"—he gave her a big hug—"welcome to the family. How come I haven't heard about this before now?" He again directed his comment to Stephen. He had released Jessica and now walked to Stephen, clasping his hand in a firm handshake. "Congrats!"

"Thanks," replied Stephen, showing very little excitement. "It just happened yesterday morning, so we couldn't very well let you know."

"Well, I guess when it comes to the really big things, your life is more private than everyone thinks. Boy howdy, are the tabloids going to have a field day with this."

"That's one reason I'd just as soon keep it quiet." Stephen smiled at Blane, but his mouth had a tight, resolute set that plainly stated that he expected his wish to be carried out.

Blane looked at his watch, saying, "It looks like it's about time." He was obviously referring to the meeting they were to attend. "I'm certainly not looking forward to this."

"Nor am I." Stephen looked decidedly grim, and Jessica wondered what the meeting could be about. He reached out and gently grabbed her arm, pulling her toward the door. "I just want to get Jessica settled in my office, and then I'll be back down and we'll go in together."

"Ah, yes," Blane smiled. "The old united-front approach. I just hope it will help."

"So do I, Blane, so do I." Stephen led Jessica through the door and down the hallway toward another room. Once inside a large, richly decorated office, Jessica asked, "Are there problems with this meeting?" The worried look on her husband's face had forced the prying question from her lips.

"Oh, nothing serious." He shrugged his shoulders. "Some of the stockholders and board members are just a little hot under the collar about some recent transactions." He placed the palm of his hand on her cheek. "Just a typical day, my love. You might as well get used to it."

It was no wonder Stephen had seemed to age so much in the last seven years. She could understand now why his eyes held a weary glaze much of the time. It wasn't easy being a successful businessman; sacrifices had to be made. She had noticed the same look in her father's eyes the last few years of his life, and she supposed that he, too, had sacrificed much to attain the stature he had.

"Sorry I have to leave you so soon, but I really do need to get down to this meeting." He was gathering up some files from the top of his desk. "Those ledgers over there on the shelf"—he pointed to some wine-colored leather-bound books on the credenza behind his desk—"they're the books for a couple of the European branches. If you want, you can go through them and familiarize yourself with the operations." He absently kissed her cheek and headed for the door. "I'll be back as soon as I can."

The door closed behind him, and Jessica was alone. She

sighed heavily, the fatigue of three days finally catching up with her. Looking around the office, she breathed in the scent of wood and leather, and the distinctive aroma of success. She walked to the window overlooking the street below.

The mist had ceased and the sky was now the color of lead. The window overlooked a park with a large stone statue in the center. Pigeons moved freely among the crowds, at home among the trees and the grass and the statue. Quite a few people were now milling about, and Jessica was surprised at the number of Arab women, veils covering their faces, who sat on blankets watching their children at play.

Jessica sighed again and moved to the credenza, picking up the leather-bound binders. She sat down in the chair behind Stephen's polished mahogany desk and, setting the books in front of her, opened one of them to the first page. Columns of figures glared back at her, and once again she felt an overwhelming lack of confidence for the role as Stephen's investor.

"Oh, excuse me." She hadn't heard the door open and she jumped at the sound of the voice speaking to her. A nice-looking, dark-haired man in his early thirties walked into the office and toward the desk. "I've just got to find a file." He was rummaging through the papers on Stephen's desk. "It's here somewhere. By the way, I'm David. David Sinclair. And you're—"

"Jessica . . . Dalheurst." She had to catch herself before she said Benchley.

"Dalheurst?" He looked mildly surprised. "I didn't know Stephen had a sister." He continued to search for the file.

"No. I'm his—" Stephen had said he wanted to keep it

quiet, but she certainly wasn't going to hide the fact. Surely he wouldn't want her to do that. "I'm his wife."

David's head raised sharply, a look of complete shock on his face. "Wife! Stephen's wife?"

"Yes. We were married yesterday morning." Was it her imagination, or had he actually looked at her stomach? Is that what people would think? That they had had to get married?

"Oh . . . well. . . . That's great. Really. Congratulations. I'm a little surprised. I just didn't know Stephen was thinking about getting married." He had extended his hand to shake hers, which she now offered to him. When the realization finally sank in, he sat down in the chair across from the desk and, it seemed to Jessica, relaxed noticeably.

"Have you known Stephen . . . long?" It was obvious that he was trying to assimilate this unexpected news.

"Yes. I've known him all my life. We grew up next door to each other."

"Really? Childhood sweethearts?" He smiled, more to himself than to Jessica. "Stephen is just full of surprises." He was scratching his head at this new bit of information.

She smiled at him and nodded. "Are you from the states?" His accent, too, was typically American.

"Yes. I'm from Atlanta, Georgia. But, I almost feel like a native. I've been in Great Britain for quite a few years."

"Whose statue is that out there?" She pointed to the window, trying to make conversation.

He looked toward the window as if trying to orient himself. "Ah, Lord Nelson."

"Oh, that must be Trafalgar Square, then." She remembered seeing pictures of that before.

"Yes."

"Do you like it here?" She was very relieved to have someone to talk to. It would make the time Stephen was gone pass much quicker.

"Oh, I suppose. I miss all of the luxuries of home. Things you Yanks take for granted. But, I like it here pretty well. There are some advantages living this close to Europe."

"I suppose so," she agreed. "I've never been there myself. But tomorrow we're going to leave for two weeks there."

"You'll love it. Stephen really knows the places to go." He was silent for a moment, as if thinking of something else to say to his boss's new wife. "Chicago," he mumbled, breaking the awkward silence. "Was Stephen ever able to convince that woman there to sell him her estate?"

"What estate?" Jessica asked politely, knowing full well that she could not answer. She still knew so little of Stephen's businesses and certainly nothing about any real estate he was wanting to purchase.

"Let's see. . . . Biltrest, Bentrest—I don't know, something like that." He shrugged.

Jessica's eyes had not left his face, and her face had not changed expression. Not an exterior muscle had moved, but inside, everything was off kilter. Her heart began pounding; her stomach felt as if it were moving up to her throat; her knees grew weak; and everything was churning. It was a long moment before she found her voice, and when she spoke, it was not above a whisper.

"Benchcrest?" she whispered, her ears roaring with confusion.

"That's it! Benchcrest," he replied nonchalantly, no idea of the explosion occurring in Jessica's mind. "Yes, as I recall, he's wanted to buy that place for quite a while."

He was waiting for her answer, but just shrugged when he didn't receive it. "I don't know any of the details, but I do know that, when Stephen sets his mind to something, nothing stops him." He stood, stretching out his hand once more to her. "I need to get back to work. I don't know what could have happened to that file. Oh, well. I'll get it later." If he was wondering why she said nothing but continued to stare at him as if in shock, he said nothing about it. Pulling back his hand, he swaggered to the door and quietly left.

Her mind was reeling; her head was throbbing. The office suddenly seemed claustrophobic. If she went outside, she wouldn't know where to go, so she moved to the window, flung open the sash, and breathed in the cool wet air. She thought she was going to throw up, but the moist air calmed her stomach slightly.

It was several minutes before she could make her mind function properly, and when it did, what she saw was not pretty. Stephen wanted to buy Benchcrest! It wasn't true. It just wasn't true! Suddenly it all came back to her. She remembered her attorney had told her three months ago that someone wanted to buy it. But Stephen! *Sell the damn place. Sell the damn place.* The memory of his words that day they went to lunch rang in her ears. He wanted her to sell it. He wanted her to sell it to him. And when she said she would never sell it—oh, God—he had decided on another solution. He had married her—for Benchcrest! As David had said, "When Stephen sets his mind to something, nothing stops him."

The pain was as sharp as if she had been stabbed by a knife and then left alone to bleed, ever so slowly, to death. Stephen had not married her for love. She knew that now, but she berated herself for not seeing it from the first.

134

Everything had happened so suddenly, so unexpectedly. When he asked her to marry him, she believed that he loved her. She had wanted to believe it. Now she knew differently: He had married her because it was the only way for him to have Benchcrest. The reason he had wanted it was not important. He had wanted it, and when Stephen Dalheurst wanted something, he got it. He had preyed upon her love for him and used her. The bottom line was that he didn't love her.

Prey. Vulture and prey. Where had she heard that before? Vultures hovering around you. . . . Suddenly she remembered: It was Thomas. Thomas had told her that. He had warned her. Why hadn't she listened? God, why hadn't she believed him!

Her thoughts were drawn back to that evening so long ago. She and her brother were in the study, Thomas working on his Ph.D. thesis, Jessica cramming for midterm exams. She had been nagging him all evening for the reason he had broken his engagement with his fiancée. Finally he had had enough.

"All right, Jessie!" he shouted in agitation. "All right! You want to know why I broke up with Suzanne? I'll tell you." He was pacing in front of the large oak desk, his fingers raking impatiently through his hair. "I found out it wasn't me she loved at all. No. You want to know what it was?" His voice was loud and strident. "It was this!" He spread his arms to encompass the house. "And this!" He pointed to the paintings on the wall. "And this!" He pulled his wallet from his pocket and threw it to the floor. "Are you happy now?"

She had not been happy. She had been ashamed that she made her brother reveal the terrible hurt he felt inside.

"You want to know what the rest of the world is like,

Jessie?" Thomas continued. He was no longer shouting, but his voice was more serious and bitter than she had ever heard it.

"It's filled with vultures . . . vultures hovering around you, just waiting to clamp their claws into your carcass. That's what money does for you. . . . It separates you from all the rest of them. And that's one thing you don't want to happen, little sister. Because when it does, you become the prey." His voice was almost a whisper now. "And they'll all be after you." *They'll all be after you . . . all be after you.*

Her head was now throbbing with the pain of truth. At the time, she had thought Thomas couldn't be more wrong about people. After all, he was just upset over the breakup with his fiancée. But now . . . now she knew how right he had been. If only she had seen it before. There had been so many clues. Even Stephen had said that everyone wants money. Even he, with all his millions, wanted still more. God, she hated him!

Time seemed to drag by as Jessica paced the office and gnawed on the painful information she had got from David. But, waiting for him to return, she was given the time to decide what she must do.

When Stephen returned from his meeting two hours later, Jessica was sitting behind his desk, absently staring at the company ledgers, and when she raised her eyes to meet his, they revealed none of the anger and hurt that was tearing her insides apart. Her face was calm and composed, her eyes unemotionally detached and vacant. She doubted if Stephen would notice, since he had just come out of a mentally exhausting meeting himself. Besides, why should he notice? He wasn't interested in her feelings anyway. She would not let on that anything was wrong, for his office was not the place for that. No, it would have to wait until they were alone. And even then he would never . . . never know the truth.

The evening dragged by just as the afternoon had, minutes ticking away, slowly and precisely. The limousine had carried them to dinner at one of Stephen's favorite local pubs and was now taking them to the apartment. When Stephen had noticed her sullen uncommunicativeness, she told him only that she was tired. It was a totally believable excuse, and he had let the subject drop.

His apartment was in an ornate four-story building, complete with dadoed columns and gargoyles and wrought-iron bars at the entrance. The interior lobby was graciously decorated; it smelled of its many years of opulence and luxury. The building spoke of old money, conservative attitudes, self-indulgence, and aristocratic demeanor. A glass-beaded chandelier hung from the center of the ceiling, casting a golden light over the marble floor partially covered by a Persian rug.

Standing behind Jessica in the elevator, Stephen slipped his arms around her waist, pulling her back against him. His mouth trailed down the back of her hair and then to her ear, his breathing soft and shallow.

"Hmm. You smell so good." His voice was slow and husky. His warm breath over her cheek sent an unwanted tingle down the center of her spine. His lips moved down to her neck, his hand lifting the hair away so that he could kiss the flesh beneath.

How much of this was an act? she wondered. He didn't really love her. Was he simply trying to make the best of a marriage that he didn't want, but that he was now stuck in? But surely there had to be some physical attraction between them. Jessica knew he couldn't be that good an actor, could he? She knew she wasn't.

She was stiff and unyielding in his arms. He stepped back slightly. "Is something wrong, Jessie?" His voice held a note of concern, but she knew it was, once again, his acting skills on display.

"No, nothing." She pulled away from him, rushing awkwardly out the open elevator door onto the fourth floor.

"Here we are," Stephen stated needlessly. They had walked to the door of his apartment, and he was using the key to open it. Once inside, Jessica's senses were assailed by the fact that this was a man's apartment. Male domination pervaded every corner, in the typically masculine decor that was expensive but casual, and in the small immaculate kitchen, whose condition attested to the fact that it was seldom used.

"I'll set your bag in the closet here, and you can do what you want with your things. You probably won't want to get too settled, since we'll be going abroad tomorrow." He set the bag down on the floor of the bedroom's large walk-in closet. "That is, unless you want to stay in England a few days." He was removing his coat and hanging it up alongside dozens of other suits evenly spaced in the closet. The bedroom was not large, but it was decorated in a style that spoke of warmth and seduction and Stephen. Jessica was still standing in the doorway, not budging an inch into the room.

"Come over here." He was seated on the bed, removing his shoes, and he patted the space beside him.

"I—I think I'll take a bath," she replied, moving to her bag in the closet. It would be so easy to go to him, to tell him that she knew. To beg him to love her or to learn to

138

love her. She would beg him, but then he would see what a fool she was. No. She had to retain her control. She would not let him know that she knew. She, too, would become a consummate actor. Her pride must be spared, for she had little else that he had not claimed. She would give him no chance to see her crushed by his loveless power. If anyone were to do the crushing, it would be she. But, right now, the idea of crushing his ego gave her little satisfaction.

Stephen patted the bed again. "I could have sworn I said, 'Come over here.' " He laughed, but Jessica saw the command inherent in his words.

"I didn't realize I was your puppy dog," she replied sarcastically, not moving from her spot in the room. She saw his eyebrows draw together in a brief frown only seconds before it was masked over by a cold hardness. She directed her eyes toward the closet, not wanting to see the dispassionate expression in his face.

"Jessica, what's wrong?" She had not heard him walking over to her, but she felt his hands on her shoulders.

"Nothing," she lied. Why didn't she say the words that she had practiced over and over again in her mind this afternoon? Why did his touch leave her so weak? His arms once again circled her from behind. And this time she could not control the sharp intake of breath as his right hand closed over her breast, his thumb arousing the nipple to a peak through her knit dress.

How was she ever going to handle this? At his touch her control and willpower completely dissolved. But she knew she mustn't give in to him. He could not dominate her—even this way. But the heat from his touch was melting her resolve.

His fingers began unfastening the buttons on the front

139

of her dress, his lips once again trailing kisses across her neck and cheek. As the dress fell open he quickly undid the clasp of her bra and her breast fell into the cup of his hand. Why didn't she stop him? Involuntarily she leaned back against the hard wall of his chest. His left hand had moved down the smooth plain of her stomach, his fingers sliding beneath the waistband of her panties. She knew she should stop him. She had to! But her mind reeled with the intoxicating scent of him, the feel of his hardened manhood behind her.

He turned her around to face him. She opened her mouth to resist, but as she did his lips clamped down on her mouth, forcing her protest to remain in her mind. His lips were gentle but demanding. His tongue forced her lips wider apart as he explored the deep crevices of her mouth. Her arms moved up around his neck, and her muscles slackened with the desire he was pulling from her. His hands were gliding across her hips, pulling them into his hardened length.

At the three sharp rings of the telephone Jessica pulled abruptly from him, turning her back on the room to fasten her bra and dress.

"Hello." Stephen's voice could not conceal the impatience he felt at the interruption. "Dan, hello. Yes. . . . Well, thank you. Yes, we're very happy. No. She's right here. Sure, just a minute." He turned to hand Jessica the phone, and her own expression revealed a curious frown. Who could be calling? Who would want to talk to her? Dan who?

"Hello?" she answered timidly. "Dan? Dan Feinstein? Well, thank you. How did you know? We didn't tell any-one. . . ." Not only was she surprised that her attorney knew that she was married, but she was shocked that he knew Stephen and his London phone number. Then she remembered that Stephen was the one who probably approached Dan with the offer to buy Benchcrest. Maybe they had plotted this thing together all along. No. She couldn't believe that Dan would do something that underhanded.

"Thank you for calling, Dan. Good-bye." When she hung up the phone, she had regained her cold resolution. She picked up her small bag and headed for the bathroom. "I'm going to take a bath now." She didn't turn to look at his expression. "It's been a very trying day." She walked into the bathroom and was closing the door when a hand reached out to stop the door from closing.

"Why don't I take one with you?" He smiled seductively.

"No," she said too quickly, the picture of such intimacy with him leaving her weak and quivering.

"I don't understand what's the matter with you, Jessie." Again the concern showed in his voice.

"No, I don't suppose you would," she hissed. Her anger surprised him; his eyes crinkled in confusion.

"For God's sake, what's the matter?" He reached out to turn her around to face him. His brown eyes had darkened until there was no distinction between pupil and iris. What was she going to say to him? How could she tell him?

She knew that the moment of truth had come. But she also knew that she would not be able to tell him the truth. "I don't love you, Stephen." His hands jerked away from her as if they had been bitten. She turned quickly so that he would not see how the falsehood had twisted her expression. If he saw her eyes, he would know that she was not telling the truth. *But I must not let him know,* Jessica thought. She waited for an interminably long minute for him to say something. She had to get this over with before she broke down sobbing in his arms and confessed her lie.

"You can't mean that, Jessica," he charged, his voice emitting a desolate, hollow sound.

No, I don't mean it, she cried inside. But then, what was he worried about? Was he concerned that Benchcrest would no longer be his? Even now, that was probably all he cared about. "Yes, Stephen. I mean it."

CHAPTER NINE

Stephen's voice did not mask the anger now. It was strident and demanding. "Did something happen this afternoon at the office?"

"No."

"So how come you were fine when I went in to the meeting . . . but when I came out, everything was changed? Did someone say something—do something—to make you feel this way?"

"What could anyone possibly say, Stephen?" She was now arrogant and haughty. Now that she had started this, she knew she would have the strength to finish it.

"Then, what? What made you change your mind?" The hollow sound had returned.

"I just don't like the world you live in. I wouldn't fit in and I don't want to fit in."

"What do you mean, 'the world I live in'?" His voice dared her to explain.

"I don't want to live in a world where money and the lust for money control people's lives."

"You think I lust for money, is that it?"

"I think—yes—lust or greed, or whatever you choose to call it, probably plays a most important role in your life." She breathed deeply before continuing. "I was happy before you barged into my life—"

"Happy!" His laugh was full of scorn. "You were happy in that cold hard shell you lived in?"

"That's right!" she shouted. "I was happy. Much happier than I am now."

He turned his back on her and began pacing the room. There was a wildness to his walk and in his face. Why didn't he just give up? Why didn't he just let her walk out of the door? When he stopped in front of her, his eyes were blazing with ferocious determination. His fingers grasped her chin, forcing her to look at him.

"Let me tell you something, Jessica *Dalheurst.*" He emphasized her married name. "I've had a lot of scandal in my life. A lot more than I care to admit. But I could handle it because it didn't really touch me personally. I could handle the names I was called by the press—and by women I had known." His mouth was tight and rigid and his words were harsh. "But I will not—I repeat, I will not—tolerate scandal in my marriage. You are my wife. You will remain my wife. And you will act like my wife."

She tried to pull her chin away from his fingers. This was not what she had expected. She thought the nightmare would be over soon, but now she realized that it was just beginning. The powerful intent in his eyes made her aware that he meant exactly what he said. She could not fight that. But she would not let him dominate her completely.

144

"All right, Stephen," she hissed. "I certainly wouldn't want to tarnish your impeccable public image." She stared at him, her nostrils flaring with anger. "You might control most of my life, but you will not have *me. I will not let you touch me.*" Her words were uttered forcefully, each one emphasized, but the pain of stating them tore at her insides.

The brown eyes that met hers were possessive and hard. "Maybe you've forgotten, little girl, that I'm you're husband. That gives me certain, shall we say, license."

She pulled her chin from his grasp, righteous anger blazing in the depths of her eyes. "What are you going to do, Stephen, rape me? You can't force me to want you, you know."

The fingers on her arm were digging into the flesh and she could feel their pressure on the bone. The mirror image of her anger flared in his eyes, the dark brown of his iris blending with the darker pupil. "As I told you before, I don't have to resort to rape to have a woman, especially my own wife." His hand moved to the back of her head, and grabbing a handful of thick brown hair, he pulled her head back, his face only inches from hers. "And I certainly don't think I would have to do much forcing to make you want me." She was stung by the scornful derision in his voice. He stared at her for a long, silent moment, then released her hair and chin from his grasp. "But I'll play your little game, Jessica. However"—his finger was pointed at her—"I expect you to play mine."

Jessica did not want to find out what would happen if she didn't play his game. Looking into the ominous power of his eyes, she felt—and not for the first time—afraid of him.

* * *

The sun was pouring through the sheer curtains of the window, illuminating the large master bedroom at Benchcrest. Jessica lay under the covers, feeling no desire to move, no desire to get up. She could hear the repetitive sounds of water hitting against the tiles of the shower, hitting against Stephen's body. She shut the thought of his body out of her mind.

The bathroom divided two bedrooms: the one she used and the one Stephen sometimes slept in. Many nights, she knew, he would fall asleep on the couch in the study, his work papers strewn across the coffee table and floor.

The honeymoon had been canceled under the pretext of business in Chicago that could not wait. After their first night in London they flew back to the states, taking a cab to Benchcrest; only when they arrived home were they free to drop their role-playing as the happily married Mr. and Mrs. Dalheurst.

The papers had what they thought was the scoop, and it—the marriage—was big news in certain circles. The newsstand tabloids revealed the "true, shocking" details of Stephen Dalheurst's marriage. She had tricked him into marriage. She had cheated on him already. She was three months pregnant. She was a deranged alcoholic. There were so many conflicting stories that Jessica finally stopped paying attention to them. She was becoming adept at her new acting role, and anyone who saw or talked to the newlyweds thought them to be blissfully happy.

The shower had stopped, and Jessica imagined Stephen's lean brown body stepping onto the bathmat, a large terry towel rubbing against his skin. Why did these thoughts constantly invade her mind? She had the powerful, restless impulse this morning—as she had so many

146

mornings—to walk into the bathroom, to press herself against the hard wall of his body. She would forgive him for marrying her only to have Benchcrest. She would forgive him for rejecting her seven years ago. She would tell him it didn't matter that he didn't love her—if only he would make love to her. If he would touch her and let her touch him. She wanted to go to him, but she did not. The years of pain and loneliness had taught her how to immobilize her emotions and her desires. She pulled back inside her shell and listened for him to leave his room.

As soon as she heard him descend the stairs she got up out of bed, showered, and put on her makeup as slowly as possible. She slipped on her jeans and a soft emerald-green velour top and headed downstairs for breakfast. It was the routine she had followed every morning for the last two weeks, and she knew every step of the way by heart.

He was seated at the dining table, the newspaper unfolded in front of him. A half-eaten biscuit, some scrambled eggs and bacon, and a glass of orange juice sat cold and uneaten on his plate. He was sipping his coffee when she walked in. Her cold smile was met by his equally detached expression.

"Good morning," she lied.

"Is it?" he asked coldly. "If you say so." He shrugged his shoulders and went back to reading his paper, ignoring her.

"I had planned for us to go into the city today," he said from behind his paper. "You said the other day you had some shopping you wanted to do." He put his paper down. "I thought we would have lunch somewhere." He was looking at her now, an unreadable expression in his eyes.

"It can wait, if you'd rather not go today." Jessica's voice was flat and expressionless. She was desperately trying to keep the emotion out of her voice. But it was very difficult. He looked so handsome this morning, so masculine in his jeans and plaid flannel shirt. It was open at the neck, his hard chest tempting her to touch it. His position was relaxed and easy. Only his face showed the strain of the tense moment.

"Are you saying you don't want to go?" he asked tersely.

Rosita pushed open the door from the kitchen, carrying a plate of breakfast and a glass of juice for Jessica.

"I hear you come down and think you might be ready to eat," she smiled nervously, looking anxiously back and forth between Stephen and Jessica. She knew things were not right. But it was better that she knew the truth now, thought Jessica. They could not have kept it from her for long.

"*Gracias,* Rosita." Jessica smiled, hoping to reassure her that things would work out, even though she knew, for herself, that they would not. Rosita did not look convinced. She backed into the kitchen, letting the door between the two rooms swing back and forth several times before finally coming to a stop.

"Well?" Stephen glared at her, waiting for the answer to his question.

"Well, what?" Jessica replied innocently, munching on a biscuit.

Stephen slammed his coffee cup to the table, uttered a harsh expletive, and stomped out of the room. A few minutes later Jessica heard the front door open and close and the engine of Stephen's Jaguar start.

When she was sure he was gone, she let the tears fall. This morning had been a repeat, with very few variations,

148

of all their mornings since they had been back from London.

How long could they keep up this masquerade? When would Stephen finally realize that they could not stay married? He had not tried to pretend any love for her at the house. Only in public did they possess the fake trappings of two people in love with each other.

Jessica's days were spent frittering about, doing nothing of consequence. She had originally thought that if and when she moved back into Benchcrest, she would redecorate the house. But now she could not muster the enthusiasm to do it. She refused even to touch the ledgers for Stephen's businesses, and so she spent her time leafing through magazines, napping, and walking about the yard.

"Jessica. . . . Is there . . . ?" Rosita's voice faltered; she felt she had no right to pry into the affairs of others.

Jessica was in the kitchen, pouring a glass of lemonade from the pitcher in the refrigerator. Hearing the concern in Rosita's voice, she set the glass on the table and sighed heavily.

"It's okay, Rosita. You deserve to know what's going on here." It wasn't as though she was merely a servant. She was a part of the family and had been ever since Jessica could remember. She had gone to Rosita often in the past when things were bothering her. Surely she could come to her now.

Jessica seated herself wearily in a chair, her elbows resting on the table and her fingertips massaging her throbbing temples. "You know why Stephen married me, don't you?"

"Ah, because he love you very much, *chiquita.*"

"No, dammit!" Jessica slammed her fist to the table. "No!" She began to cry, and as the tears fell Rosita

149

wrapped her fleshy arms around Jessica and held her tightly to her breast, comforting her as if she were a little girl once again. "He married . . . me . . . just . . . just to have this house." She was sobbing as she spoke, the words uttered chokingly between tears.

"No!" Rosita did not believe such a thing of Stephen. "No. Señor Stephen would not do such a thing!" She had known him too long, ever since he was a little boy. He was not that kind of man. But Jessica was shaking her head, assuring Rosita that he would, that he did; that was exactly what he had done.

When Jessica's tears were spent, Rosita pulled away to sit in a chair beside her. Her kind, round face and soft, gentle eyes were a comfort to Jessica, and she suddenly felt less alone, less frightened. Even if she had no one else, she at least had Rosita. Managing a weak smile, she said "He did, Rosita. I know. I found out. That's the only reason he married me."

"Did Señor Stephen tell you this?"

"No."

"Then who did?"

"It was one of the people who works for him in London. He told me." She didn't try to hide the bitterness she felt as she remembered that day in Stephen's office.

"You must have misunderstood, Jessica," Rosita insisted, but Jessica shook her head. "You asked Stephen if this was true?"

"No. He mustn't know that I know." She grabbed Rosita's arm, a frantic look in her eyes. "You mustn't tell him that I know. Promise me!"

"*Sí* . . . I promise. . . . But don't you think you should talk to him. Maybe if—"

"No. We're through talking. The marriage is—over."

She nervously passed her glass of lemonade from one hand to the other. "Stephen's got to see that. I'm just waiting for him to realize it and give up. But he's so—so stubborn . . . so . . . I don't know." She felt so tired, so defeated.

"*Sí*, Señor Stephen has always been like that, so sure he is right. Ever since he was little boy, no?" Rosita smiled and Jessica nodded wistfully. "But then, so have you, Jessica. You and Stephen are—how you say—two pea pods?"

"Two peas in a pod," Jessica corrected as she stared into her glass of lemonade.

"*Sí*, that's what I say. Two pea pods." Jessica's mouth quirked into a smile. "Ever since you two were little, you were always getting into trouble. Now, Tomás, he was different. He was so good and never any trouble. He always did what I said. But you and Stephen, ha!" Rosita shook her head and rolled her eyes, remembering the frustration of trying to discipline them.

Jessica lay her head on the table, resting her eyes in the crook of her arm. Why couldn't she go back to those days of her youth when everything was so simple, so uncomplicated? Why did life have to be so difficult?

By the afternoon she was feeling a little better. She had at least confided in Rosita and now no longer had to pretend in front of her. Grabbing a light sweater, she went for a walk in the yard.

Suddenly spring was here. She hadn't noticed it creeping up on her. She had been so wrapped up in her own problems that she had not noticed the quivering burst of new life. She breathed in the sweet smell of the air, but it did not sweeten the bitterness she felt inside. She stopped at one of the flower beds, stopping to grab a handful of the rich, brown dirt. She let it sift through her fingers, feeling the coolness where it touched her hand. A few crocuses were starting to sprout, the shining green leaves thrusting from the imprisonment of the dirt.

Wiping her hand on her jeans, she walked leisurely through the trees, her nostrils filled with the woodsy smell. She passed through the woods, coming out near the lake. The sun shimmered across the water, and Jessica felt compelled to stand at the edge, daring the Fates and gravity to pull her down the steep rocky wall. There were no tears now; she had shed them all this morning.

She turned to look at the house and saw him walking toward her. He was coming straight down from the house, pausing at the tennis courts to pick up a stray ball. She noticed that he was still wearing the flannel shirt and jeans he had on this morning. He looked warm and casual—and so damn masculine. Blatant virility radiated from his carefree stride and from the slightly arrogant set of his head. Why did she have to love him so? Why did he have to be so good-looking? Why did his presence automatically set her nerves on edge with erotic impulses?

As he drew nearer she once again wanted to run to him and throw herself against his lean, hard body. But the survival instinct and the years of emotional control kept her feet firmly rooted to the spot where she was standing.

Stopping only a foot in front of her, Stephen's eyes held a look of detachment.

"You had better go get dressed," he stated casually. "We are going out tonight."

"Oh?" she replied sarcastically. "And who decided this?"

"I did. We're going to meet some friends at Second City, and then go have some drinks afterward." He was looking out across the water, avoiding her haughty expression.

"I suppose I don't have any say in the matter, do I?" she huffed.

"Not a bit." He looked at her with a cold, vacant stare.

Jessica wore a flattering peach-colored blouse and black silk pants. It gave her a sensual appeal and enhanced her own beautiful complexion. She knew she looked good, but she doubted if Stephen would even notice. Did she really care if he did or not?

The friends of Stephen were already at Second City when they got there, and Jessica was surprised to see Angela with one of the men.

"Angela! What on earth are you doing here?" She hugged her friend.

"I have a date with this unbelievably sexy man here." Angela looped her arm through her date's, a seductive smile curving her lips.

"Well, it's great to see you." Jessica had to admit that Angela had a way of making men putty in her hands. She had mixed feelings about her being there though. It was good to see her friend again, but she didn't want her to notice any problems between Stephen and herself. And if anyone could see through this ridiculous charade, it would be Angela.

"I haven't seen you since you got married," Angela smiled. "I knew you were holding back on me. I just knew it." Jessica's eyes involuntarily flew to Stephen's face, meeting his steady gaze. "Pretending you didn't have anything going with this guy," Angela scoffed and smiled at Stephen. Stephen's smile for Angela was relaxed and affectionate, and Jessica felt a momentary flash of jealousy.

The first part of the evening at Second City passed quickly. She always enjoyed coming to this improvisation theater, where some of the popular comedians of the day had got their start. She laughed and enjoyed the fun with everyone else, forgetting for a little while the troubles that were plaguing her marriage and her life. Stephen seemed to be enjoying himself too. And Jessica noticed more than once the easy rapport he had with Angela. They would laugh and joke together as if they had been friends for a long time, rather than just having met tonight. For the first time Angela's outgoing personality annoyed Jessica, and she found herself wishing that Stephen could laugh that easily with her instead. But it was not possible. There were too many lies, too much deceit, and too little love between them.

When the actors took a break, Jessica and Angela went to the powder room. Standing in front of the wide mirror, Angela swooned. "Oh, Jessica, he *is* wonderful. I'm so jealous."

"Of what?" Jessica asked, trying to feign lack of interest.

"Of what! Of you, silly. He's gorgeous," she exclaimed, referring to Stephen. "And he is so much fun to be with too."

"Yes—yes, he is," Jessica lied casually, applying lipstick to her mouth.

"I bet he's great in other departments too." Angela brushed her hair back off her face, casually patting it into place.

"Angela!" Jessica was indignant.

"Okay. Sorry." Her hands were at her shoulders in a position of surrender. "I should have known you wouldn't indulge me with any delicious family secrets." They headed out of the powder room together with Angela adding, "I can tell he really loves you, Jessica. You can see it in his eyes every time he looks at you."

Jessica's face hid the emotional turmoil produced by her friend's comment. How could Angela be so blind? Surely she could see through this ridiculous masquerade. Surely she could tell that Stephen did not care a thing about her, except as another piece of his property. It would be wonderful, thought Jessica, if what Angela said were true. But there wasn't much point in dwelling on it; it was nothing more than an empty fantasy.

At the nightclub later, she was forced, out of politeness, to dance with each of the men. And she could not help but notice that Stephen was dancing more than necessary with Angela. Did she actually see his hand caressing her back as they danced? But then, why should she care if he did? The drinks had been flowing heavily, and she could tell that he had drunk too much. When they said good-bye to the others around midnight, she tried to watch dispassionately as Stephen kissed Angela good night. He kissed the other girls, too, but it seemed to Jessica as if he put a little too much into the one he gave Angela.

"Do you want to just spend the night at the town house instead of driving back tonight?" His words were slightly slurred, and she noticed that the car was already driving toward the townhouse anyway.

"It doesn't really matter," she answered flatly.

"No. I guess it doesn't, does it." As the car squealed around a corner she looked at his face. It was hard and full of scorn, and the muscles of his jaw were moving convulsively.

Once in the town house, she remembered that there was

only one bedroom. Well, since it was his idea to come here, he could just sleep on the couch. Jessica headed straight for the bedroom and turned to close the door behind her when the doorway was blocked by Stephen's large frame.

"What were you planning to do, lock me out?" His voice was low and ominous.

"Do I need to?" Her voice was slightly shaky.

His gaze traveled slowly and seductively over her legs and hips and breasts, lingering momentarily at the top button of her blouse. When his eyes hooked on her face, he took a step into the room.

"What are you doing?" she asked warily. She didn't trust him. He had had too much to drink tonight, and his eyes held a dangerous, haunted look.

His hand reached out, his fingers lightly touching her cheek. Then they began to pull gently on the fringe of her hair. When she jerked her head away from his touch, his hand closed around the strands of hair pulling her toward him. His mouth was inches from her and she could smell the alcohol on his breath. "I'm claiming what's mine"—his voice throbbed huskily—"that's what I'm doing."

Before she could speak, his mouth seized hers, his lips grinding hard against her teeth. His arms circled around her, holding her fast to his chest. She whimpered and tried to move away, but his mouth kept pressing harder against her, his tongue forcing its way between her teeth. When she thought she would surely black out from the pressure on her lungs and mouth, he loosened his hold, his mouth moving to her neck to kiss the sensitive skin there. Her hands were between them, pushing against his chest, her body struggling to free itself.

"No, Stephen. No!" She pushed hard and was suddenly

free of his embrace. His eyes were blazing with desire and anger. But she saw a flash of pain dart across the planes of his face then disappear into the hard frozen mask.

"You're my wife, dammit!" he hissed. His hand was grasping the edge of the door, his knuckles white against the wood, his shoulders rigid and taut.

She wanted him. God, how she wanted him! But not this way. She couldn't live with herself if she surrendered to this kind of demand. She would never escape him, and her own self-esteem would drown in the physical control he would hold over her. She clutched her hands in front of her, holding them still as she steadied her eyes on his face.

"Only on paper, Stephen. I am your wife *only* on paper."

With a lightening swiftness that left her stunned, Stephen had grabbed her and thrown her down on the bed. One hand held her wrists above her head while the weight of his body pinned her against the mattress.

"You're lying!" His voice was filled with a mixture of anguish and incredible anger. "I know you're lying! You want me as badly as I want you." She was throwing her head from side to side, trying to escape his clutches, but the feel of his hard body on hers was distracting, and she couldn't control the weakening in her limbs.

"No! I don't want you. I—"

"Stop fighting me, Jessica. Dammit, I won't let you do this to us!" He had unbuttoned her blouse and removed his own shirt and his skin raked against her breasts. At the contact an electric jolt shattered her nerves.

"Stephen, please!" she begged, not sure what she was begging for. But when his mouth closed over hers, parting her lips with possessive demand, and the blood swept like fire through her veins, she knew what she was begging for. She wanted him. She hated herself for wanting him, but she knew she couldn't go another day without his possession. The ache inside was too strong, too agonizing to subdue. She would not be able to talk away the pain this time.

She continued to fight for escape, but her body betrayed her with every move, and in her mind, she knew she had already surrendered.

It was over. The fire was now only an ember, glowing in a bed of ashes. But the ache of longing that she had felt for him, for his body, for his touch, was overshadowed by the unbelievable pain of self-disgust that she was now feeling. Why had she done it? Why had she let him do this? No. Why had she *wanted* him to make love to her? That was the question. She had wanted him and, worse still, she had let him know that she wanted him. God, what a fool she was! She had let him take the last shred of dignity that she had left. She would never forgive him for that.

Yet, she knew that she would, that she already had. For as he lay there asleep, his arm draped across her stomach, she knew that she loved him and that, no matter what he did, she would forgive him. And that fact alone filled her with disgust.

She slipped quietly from beneath his arm and tiptoed into the bathroom to dress. She had to get out of here, get away from him, before he woke. She couldn't bear to look at him, to have him look at her and see the weakness in her eyes. Because then he would hate her too. After all, he didn't marry her for love. She had to remember that. He had married her for Benchcrest. She couldn't let him know that he had taken everything from her. He had already taken her virginity, her house, her acquiescence in his little scheme to appear happily married. She couldn't let him know that he had now taken her self-esteem too.

After she had dressed, she slipped back into the bedroom and picked up her purse on the chair. She had turned the doorknob and was silently opening the door when he spoke.

"Jessica?" He jumped from the bed and walked quickly over to the door where she was standing. It took all the effort she could muster to control her breathing as she watched the play of light on his lean, tanned body. He was gorgeous; she couldn't deny it. And she would probably always feel this uncontrollable desire for him, but—but she would not give in to those desires again. She couldn't!

"Where are you going?" he asked as his hands gently grasped her upper arms.

"Well, this has been fun, Stephen, but don't expect this to change anything." She prayed that her face reflected a composure she was not feeling inside.

"Fun?" He looked dazed. "Fun!" he repeated through clenched teeth. His hands had tightened their grip on her arms, his fingers curling into her flesh painfully. "Is that what this was to you? Fun?" The intense heat from his eyes frightened her, but she refused to be daunted.

"As I said last night before you forced—" She drew in a deep breath. "As I said, I am your wife only on paper. Don't expect anything else." She turned her head quickly to hide the tears that were forming there. *God, Stephen, don't let me say these things to you! Make me tell you I love you!*

In devastating silence she heard him dress. Then he was standing in front of her, looking at her, but she could not look at him. She kept her face turned toward the floor and watched as his feet carried him out the front door.

When the door closed and she was left alone in the bedroom, her body slumped onto the bed in a sobbing heap.

CHAPTER TEN

He was gone. And Jessica had to admit that she was relieved. But it was a painful relief all the same. The last few weeks had been a nightmare, and she had been in a continuous state of suffocation. Since that night in town, she and Stephen had avoided each other at all costs. He slept on the couch in the study and was gone in the morning long before she came down to breakfast. He rarely came home for meals, usually returning late at night after she had retired to her own room. He had not tried to touch her again since that night at the town house.

Rosita walked around the house, wringing her hands constantly. Jessica could tell that she was upset by this estrangement and by the fact that she could say or do nothing to either of them that would heal the wounds. If they were children again, she could take them in her arms and talk to them, scold them, make them talk to each other. But now there was nothing, nothing that she could do to help.

Jessica was beginning to wonder how long she could take this pervading gloom in the house when Stephen announced that he would be leaving for Europe. He did not know how long he would be gone and gave no explanation of his plans there. He told Jessica at dinner and was gone before she awoke the next morning.

Though relieved that the awkward avoidance of each other was no longer necessary, Jessica was soon wrapped in an oppressive despondency. She moved through the days without direction, without plans, and without enthusiasm. She knew she had to do something to lift herself out of this depression.

A week after Stephen left for Europe, Jessica said her good-byes to Rosita and Hernando and moved back into the house in town. Luckily it was still furnished, and she had only to move her clothes and personal items.

Holding Mr. Caldwell to his promise of a job, she found herself back in the same position she had been in only a couple of months before—almost.

So many things had changed, and inside she was a different person. The shell that had taken so many years to build had an irreparable crack. Her nights were filled with a desperate longing for Stephen, a tormenting ache in the pit of her stomach, throbbing for his touch, his lips, his body. Though she despised him and what he had done to her, she missed him desperately, but she knew that it was better this way. She was free of him and he was now free of her. His little scheme to own Benchcrest didn't work, but at least he was no longer forced to pretend an undying love for her.

Her excuse for returning to work was that Stephen was away on business, and she simply needed the work to keep her busy. She didn't volunteer any information about their problems, and no one asked.

She worked hard to make new customers and keep up with the latest changes in the market. The Dow Jones averages had once again reached that magic number: one thousand. The entire financial community was in a state of euphoria, and the investment business was booming. But Jessica just could not regain her excitement for it. She plodded through the monotonous days with dogged resolution, never capturing the investment fever she once had. Only Bill seemed to ease her misery.

"Jessica?" She was in Marshall Field's at lunchtime, doing some shopping, when she heard his voice.

"Bill!" Her smile was affectionate but slightly guilty. "I'm so glad to see you."

"Well . . ." He seemed a little restrained but welcoming. "I'm glad to see you too. I haven't seen you since you— since you got married."

What must he think of me? Jessica wondered. She never told him she was getting married or was married. He must have found out by reading it in the papers.

"Bill, I'm sorry. I should have told you. It just happened so suddenly."

"Yeah. . . . Well, that's okay." Always the gentleman, Jessica reflected. Good old Bill would never let on that he was hurt or angry. "Is Stephen here with you?"

"No," she said a little too quickly.

He glanced at her with a curious look. "Are you living in the town house or where?" They were blocking the way to the escalator, and Bill took her elbow and pulled her to the side.

"Yes . . . I'm . . . living there. Stephen is— He is in Europe." She averted her eyes so that Bill would not see

163

the tears forming there. She didn't want to break down in front of him. She didn't want anyone to know, anyone to feel sorry for her.

"Jessica?" His hand gently touched her upper arm. "Is everything okay?"

The tears were falling and she couldn't speak. She didn't want to cry. Why couldn't she hold them back?

"Come on. Let's walk." He was holding her next to him, his arm around her shoulder as they walked through the department store and out onto Michigan Avenue. They crossed the street against the traffic and began walking through Grant Park. It was a beautiful day, the kind of spring day that brings everyone outside for lunch. Grant Park was especially beautiful at this time of year, and Jessica often enjoyed walking through here during her lunch break. But today she could not stop the tears. They kept falling as quickly as she could wipe them away.

Bill found a vacant bench and he helped her sit down. He held both her hands until she finished crying and then in a gentle demand said, "Tell me what's wrong, Jessica."

She hardly knew where to begin. But the words, the accusations, the hurt, the recriminations, began pouring out until soon the whole story—except for that night in the town house together—had been told. There was a long pause after she finished speaking.

"Damn him!" Bill snarled, his harsh voice full of loathing. He was more angry than she had ever seen him before. But those two words were all he said about it. He never again brought up Stephen's name, and Jessica never volunteered another word about him.

They began seeing more and more of each other. Bill was the one person with whom she could relax and be herself. It was as though their relationship took off where they had left it. It was still easygoing, safe, and without emotional commitment. And she was grateful that he didn't plague her again with questions about her marriage.

Jessica tried to keep busy. She spent long hours at the office and several evenings a week with Bill. But at night, when she was alone in her own bed, she would let go of her emotions. The tears would fall until her pillow was soaked and until she was left with only the lonely, dull ache in the pit of her stomach. Some nights she would lie in bed until light broke across the horizon and she would wonder what Stephen was doing and whom he was with, and she would yearn for his body next to hers.

April fourteenth was a day that would be permanently etched in Jessica's memory, for it was the day that marked a new beginning in her life.

It actually began the night before when she met Bill after work for dinner.

"Where do you want to eat tonight?" Bill's question was the usual one. He had asked it each night they had gone to dinner, and they would spend a cheerful half hour eliminating the possibilities. But tonight, Jessica couldn't muster her same enthusiasm.

"Oh, it doesn't really matter," she answered with indifference.

"Is everything okay?" he asked, his voice filled with concern.

"Yes. Everything's fine." But it wasn't. She had been feeling lethargic for several days and, even with Bill, she couldn't shake the loneliness she felt without Stephen. But she certainly couldn't tell Bill that. She didn't want his pity. She wanted his company and his friendship. She wanted someone to make her forget Stephen. She wanted a man.

He looked at her with a thoughtful, tender expression, and she knew in that moment that he loved her. She didn't want him to, but she knew that he did. Sweet, kind Bill. Why couldn't she have been in love with him? Why did she have to love someone who didn't love her? Life wasn't supposed to be this complicated. When she was young, she had thought that everything would fall into a pattern, that life would order itself. What had gone wrong? She had grown up and found that life and happiness were not mail-order easy. She had been born with a silver spoon in her mouth, but now, approaching her twenty-seventh birthday, she found the silver to be tarnished and bitter to the taste.

"Well, let's go to Gino's tonight," Bill decided, putting at least this part of her life into orderly perspective. "Neither one of us really wants to dress up anyway."

"That sounds fine," she smiled.

The lasagna was delicious, as usual, and they ordered a small pizza to share. They were seated in a back corner of the subterranean restaurant. Bill had ordered a carafe of wine and was now raising his glass in the air.

"I have a toast to make." His voice was outrageously official.

"You do?" she asked with surprise. It was so unlike Bill to become ceremonious over things. Her curiosity was definitely piqued.

He cleared his throat officiously. "Yes. Today I"—the glass was lowered slowly and the humble familiarity returned to his face—"I made partner in the firm," he finished in a soft voice.

"Bill, that's wonderful." She was really very happy for

166

him. To make partner in a large accounting firm was a major achievement in itself and to make it at such a young age was almost unheard of. "I'm so happy for you. This really is an occasion to celebrate."

His expression turned serious, and his voice remained low and secretive. "It would be even more of an occasion to celebrate if—" He paused, uncertain of what he should say. "I'm going to be taking a couple of weeks off from work, and I was thinking about going to the Virgin Islands and— Well, it would be really nice if you'd go with me, Jessica." Seeing her mouth open in immediate protest, he pleaded, "Don't make a decision yet, just think about it for a little while. I'll—I'll order some more wine."

Jessica watched Bill as he signaled the waitress and ordered another carafe of wine. They had not even made a dent in the one they had, but she didn't want to protest too much. She had not meant for this to happen. She wanted a man, but not to love her; she had no room in her heart to love anyone but Stephen. When she had gone to Bill's office that afternoon, she had wanted to be with someone who respected her and made her feel like a woman. But she hadn't meant for him to become this serious about her. She had tried to keep their relationship on a friendly basis. Had she unintentionally led him on?

They finished the meal without returning to the subject of Bill's trip. She could tell he was making an effort to keep the conversation light and friendly. But she couldn't stop the queasy tightness in her stomach. Why couldn't they have kept the relationship the way it was? Why did love have to play a part in it? Love, like money, had a tendency to destroy perfectly good relationships.

"What do you want to do now?" They had just left the

restaurant and were walking through the chaotic nightlife of Rush Street.

"I think I'd like to go home now, Bill. It was so hectic at work today, and I'm really tired."

"You don't want to talk about it, do you?" Bill had stopped in the middle of the sidewalk, his hand resting gently on Jessica's shoulder.

"Bill—"

"I mean, you don't want the relationship—our relationship—to change. I'm right, aren't I, Jessica?" They were standing there facing each other, oblivious to the other pedestrians.

"I don't know. I—" Jessica suddenly felt very foolish standing in the open discussing something so personal. "Can we walk?"

They walked to the corner parking lot, where Bill had left his car. After Bill started the engine, they drove the few blocks to Jessica's apartment in silence. Parking at the curb in front of her house, Bill jumped out of the car and walked to her door to help her out. He held her hand as they walked to the front door.

"Why don't you come in for a minute." Bill had unlocked the door to her house and handed her the key.

"No." His voice was reluctant. "No. I don't think so." They were standing there awkwardly, neither one knowing what to do next.

"Jessica, I can't continue like this." Bill's voice had a painful, hoarse sound to it. "I need someone too. Someone who needs me for more than—than just friendship."

She started to speak, but he waved his hand in the air and said, "No wait, let me finish. I've never told you I loved you before because I didn't want to rush you or pressure you into something you weren't ready for. But I do—love you. God, Jessica! You drive me crazy."

Jessica had never seen him this way before, his eyes so filled with emotion, and she was sorry for what she had done to him.

"I've wanted to touch you so often," he continued. "But dammit, you've got this wall around you that I just can't seem to penetrate. I've tried to understand, tried to be patient. I thought maybe Dalheurst hurt you so badly that you needed lots of time for the wounds to heal. But I—I just don't think I can wait much longer. I'm not getting any younger and I need some sort of commitment."

"Bill, I—"

"Jessica, please don't say anything now. Just think about it."

"But, Bill—"

"Please. Please think about it overnight. Tomorrow I'll meet you after work and we can talk about it more then. Just do this one thing for me. Please, Jessica."

She owed him that much. He had given her so much in the way of friendship and emotional strength, and she had given him so little. This time, she would do something for him. She would think about it as he had asked. "All right, Bill. I'll . . . think about it."

She did think about it, although from the beginning she had known what the answer was. She didn't love Bill. She loved Stephen. She had been very unfair to Bill if she had led him to think otherwise. She just hoped that telling him the truth would not sever their friendship.

She did not sleep well that night, worrying about Bill's feelings, berating herself for leading him on, longing for the feel of Stephen's body next to hers. Morning came too soon and with it the anxiety of having to meet her attorney. A few days before, after much soul-searching, she had made a major decision, but she needed his advice before she followed through with it.

She walked past the receptionist into the plush office.

"Hello, Dan."

"Good morning, Jessica. Sit down. Can I get you some coffee?"

"No, thanks," she answered. While Dan sipped at the steaming coffee his secretary brought him, Jessica looked from her chair out the window at the panoramic view of the city. The view from this side of the pyramid-shaped Hancock Building was straight west, miles of high rises and low-lying houses that dropped off suddenly to meet the plains.

"Things will certainly be a lot easier now that you and Stephen are married," Dan was saying. Jessica frowned slightly, trying to understand what he meant by that. "I've followed Stephen's instructions to a T for so many years though, that I'm going to have to revise all of my thinking and my files."

Followed Stephen's instructions! What was Dan talking about? She had come here to talk to him about selling Benchcrest. She had thought she would never sell the house, but after what Stephen had done just to obtain it, she convinced herself that the house would never mean what it once did to her. By selling it, she would not only have her revenge against Stephen, but she would also never have to go there again and face the painful lies about their marriage. It was a difficult decision, one of the hardest she had ever had to make, but one which she thought was probably the best she could make under the circumstances.

"Now, what was it you wanted to talk about?" Dan was

pushing his files and papers to the side to make space in front of him.

"I'm thinking about selling Benchcrest. And . . . well, I just thought I should talk to you about it before I did it." She watched Dan's coffee cup stop in midair, moving neither to his mouth nor to the desk.

"Does Stephen want to sell it?" He seemed genuinely surprised by her intentions, his forehead wrinkling in a frown.

"I don't think Stephen has anything to do with it, Dan." Jessica was perturbed at his question and did not hide the fact. Why should she have to get Stephen's permission to sell her own house?

"Well, of course he does, Jessica. You can't sell the house without Stephen's permission." The coffee cup returned to the desk.

"It's my house!" she argued. "Why on earth should I have to get Stephen's permission?" This was outrageous! It was the 1980s. A woman didn't have to have her husband's permission to sell her own property.

"Jessica . . . I thought, since you were married now, that you knew." He paused as if trying to decide whether to continue. "You don't own Benchcrest."

"What!" Her exclamation snapped in the tense air.

"Stephen owns Benchcrest. He has for nine years."

"What are you saying?" Her breath was now coming in short gasps, her mind reeling with incomprehension.

"I thought that by now you knew." Dan looked nervously around the room. He closed his eyes briefly and expelled a long sigh. "I'm saying that you don't have any money—other than what you make at the brokerage firm." Dan's voice was soft and sympathetic. "You have

171

no estate. Stephen has been funding your bank account for years."

"I don't believe you," she growled angrily. "My father and mother had a very large estate."

"Your father was broke, Jessica. I'm sorry to have to break this to you. I've kept it a secret for so long. I just assumed that Stephen would have told you by now. Before your parents died they were living on credit and personal loans from the Dalheursts."

"You're lying!" Jessica burst from her chair and began pacing the room, her heart racing in response to her vexation.

"I am not lying, Jessica." Dan's voice was tender but emphatic.

"But I was under the impression that Stephen wanted to buy Benchcrest." She stopped in the middle of the room, puzzling over how all of the information fit together.

"That's true." Dan's hands were clasped in front of him on the desk. "He wanted me to approach you with the idea of selling it. You hadn't lived there for six years, so he naturally thought you were not that attached to the place." He paused before continuing. "He thought if he could pay you for it, you would have enough money to live on without finding out that you were . . . broke." The last word was uttered softly, hiding the harshness of its meaning.

"You mean, he would buy it even though he already owned it?" The idea was almost too much to comprehend.

"Yes."

"Why would he do that for me?"

"He's a good man, Jessica. I don't care what the papers say about him; he's a decent, kind man. And he never wanted you to have to find out that he was financing you. He never wanted you to feel that you owed him anything."

"You mean my education, the repairs on Benchcrest, all my expenses, have been paid by Stephen?" She was still trying to absorb this bizarre bit of information.

"That's right. Luckily for him, you have chosen to live simply. You never squandered money or lived frivolously. But . . . I suppose even if you had, he would have paid for it." He smiled at her. "I'm sorry I had to tell you. I just assumed—since you're married—that he would have told you himself."

"No . . . no, he didn't."

"Maybe he thought if you were married, he would never have to tell you. Damn!"

"Don't be sorry, Dan. I'm glad you told me." Wasn't it always best to know the truth? she thought. "It clears up quite a few things that have been bothering me. Thank you."

After leaving the attorney's office, Jessica walked and walked and walked. She walked up and down streets, around blocks, never knowing where she was going or for how long she had been walking. She had to think. She had to clear away the cobwebs in her brain.

Everything made much more sense now. The reason Stephen wanted Benchcrest, the reason he had stopped by to see the house frequently, and even the reason he had switched his investment account to Jessica. Even then he was trying to help her out on money. And she had told him that she didn't need his money! God, what a fool she had been.

Why did he do it? Why did he keep it from her all these years? Dan said he was a decent man, and she had to believe that now. But surely there had to be something more. Could he possibly have loved— No, she couldn't even begin to hope for that.

And, besides, she had blown any chance of them making their marriage work. She had told him that she didn't love him, that she wouldn't fit into his world. She had even accused him of being greedy and lusting after money. How could she have been so stupid! So cruel! He was probably the most unselfish man she had ever known.

Perhaps it had been an obligation to him. Yes. That was probably it. And Stephen certainly wasn't one to shirk responsibility. If she was nothing more than an obligation to him—which, she had to admit, she probably was—then maybe that was why he had married her. After all, he was already financing her. Why not marry her and make it legitimate?

The pain of thinking that she was a burden to him, simply another in a long line of obligations, tore at her insides like the razor-edged blade of a knife.

What was she going to do? She loved him; that she couldn't deny. But if he didn't love her . . . no! She couldn't think that. She would make him love her. She would tell him that it didn't matter if he did now or not. She had enough love for both of them.

As she rounded the corner of Grand and Michigan for the third or fourth time, she saw him. He was across the street in front of the Tribune Building. One hand was pressed flat against the stone building as he leaned his body against it. The other was in his left pocket.

Her heart began beating wildly at the sight of him. She hadn't expected this kind of luck. This was her opportunity to tell him, to go to him. She was just about to cross the street, to run to him, to throw her arms around him and tell him how sorry she was, to beg his forgiveness, to tell him she loved him. But, before crossing through traffic, she stopped. She noticed that he was not alone. He was talking to someone much shorter than he, and Jessica couldn't see who it was.

And then, suddenly, that person stepped away from him and headed for the door of the Tribune lobby. It was Angela! Angela with Stephen! Jessica watched her turn and smile that seductive smile at him before entering the building. He ran his fingers through his hair and smiled back. Oh, God, not Stephen and Angela! She had lost him. She had really lost him for good. And to her best friend.

She had not been imagining things that night at Second City. They *had* been attracted to each other. And in the powder room Angela had tried to worm out personal information about him. She probably knew him more intimately than Jessica did.

Without realizing it, she had pressed herself flat against the wall of the building, pushing hard to make herself invisible. She couldn't let Stephen see her here. She couldn't let him know that she knew. Her face was pale, her eyes vacant and cavernous, but she did not notice the curious stares of the people passing her on the sidewalk. In a daze she watched Stephen head north on Michigan Avenue and disappear in the crowd of pedestrians.

CHAPTER ELEVEN

She did not go back to work that afternoon. She did not even call in to the office. Instead, she walked for hours on end, thinking and crying and cursing and crying and re-thinking. She was frightened, and she was hurt, and she was angry. But she had come to a decision.

It was the most painful decision she had ever had to make in her life, but she knew that it was the right one.

She loved Stephen, and she would for as long as she lived. She knew there would be no one else for her. Not Bill. Not anyone. And her first impulse had been to tell Stephen that she loved him, to tell him that she knew what he had done for her all these years, to tell him that she would make no demands on him. She would not force him to love her if only he wouldn't leave her.

That had been her second and third impulses also. But she was wrong. She had no right to do that to him. She had been an obligation to him for so many years, and he had never complained. She would be a burden no more.

He was entitled to the type of life he wanted, the woman he wanted. She loved him, but she had to let him go. It sounded so simple. Why did it feel as if her very life were being ripped from her?

She was sitting on the couch in her town house, staring at the cold logs in the fireplace. Even the knock at the door did not penetrate the shroud covering her mind. Finally the knocking became louder and more insistent, and she reacted to the sound.

"Bill!" She had forgotten about him. She was supposed to meet him after work. What time was it now? She had completely lost track of everything.

"Jessica, are you all right? Damn, I was really worried. You weren't at the office, and they said you hadn't come back since lunch." He stopped, his eyes narrowing to scrutinize her appearance. "You look terrible!"

"Thanks." She responded with no humor.

"I mean you look— Is everything okay? Did something happen? Dalheurst—did he do something?"

"No, Bill. I mean yes. I don't know. I'm so confused." She turned her back on him as he stood awkwardly inside the still open door.

"You mean about last night?" he asked hopefully.

Last night? What did he mean, 'last night'? Then she remembered: the commitment he wanted. She hadn't thought about him or their talk since this morning. Was it really only last night that they had had that discussion? It seemed so long ago, a part of another lifetime. "No, Bill . . . not about last night."

"Then what? Have you decided . . . thought about . . ."

"Bill," she interrupted, wanting to get this over with. "I can't . . . commit myself to you—to anyone." Bill's hands

177

were thrust nervously into his pockets, and Jessica stood by the couch, her fingers absently toying with the nubby texture of the Haitian cotton.

She moved over to him, placing a soft hand on his forearm just below the elbow. "I love Stephen. I'm sorry, Bill."

"I see." His voice was dry and flat.

"I don't think you do." She pulled her hand away. "I'm going to give him a di-divorce." The word caught in her throat. "But that doesn't change the way I feel about him. Please try to understand. I never meant for you to fall in love with me. I never meant to—hurt you."

Bill's hand reached up behind her head, his fingers lightly stroking her hair. "It does hurt, Jessica. It hurts like hell. But I think I was expecting this. And I am a grown man." His other hand lifted to cup her cheek. "But you'll always have a friend to come to if you need one."

"Thank you, Bill." His lips descended to kiss hers. It was a gentle, loving kiss that stamped their relationship as friends forever.

"Well, isn't this cozy?" The harsh, derisive voice cut through the air like a knife. Bill and Jessica jumped apart at the sound.

"Stephen!" Her hand flew to her lips in surprise, as she saw him filling the doorway with his frame. He was dressed in brown corduroy slacks, his beige and blue shirt open at the neck, and his honey-colored hair was carelessly disarrayed as if he had just pushed his fingers through the gold strands. But his eyes blazed with an anger beyond anything Jessica had ever seen.

"Don't bother covering your mouth," he sneered sarcastically. "I saw the whole thing."

"I don't think you did see the whole thing." Jessica was amazed at the calm, even tone in Bill's voice.

"Shut up, Bill." Stephen fired at the other man, but his eyes never left Jessica's face. "I ought to kill you," he whispered angrily, and Jessica wasn't sure whom he was directing the threat to. The intention of the threat became obvious when Stephen took a few steps toward Bill. "If I ever catch you near my wife again—I'll kill you. Get out of here."

If Bill was afraid of Stephen, he somehow kept it hidden. A lesser man would have been cowering under the dominant strength and size of a man like Stephen. But Bill calmly turned to Jessica to see what she wanted him to do.

"Bill, maybe you had better go." She was still shocked to see Stephen, but she was no longer afraid of him.

Bill paused a moment, trying to decide if she would be all right, then said "Okay, but remember what I said, Jessica. If you ever—"

"Get out!" Stephen's voice roared above Bill's.

With one last glance of concern at Jessica, Bill left quietly, closing the door behind him.

The minute Jessica had seen Stephen, her heart began a wild staccato beat. The mere sight of him sent her blood boiling through her veins. Why was he here? What could he possibly want? Her blood chilled at the sudden thought of what she had to do, of what she had to say to him.

Stephen was breathing heavily, his jaw flexing in anger. "So this is what you do when I go out of town." His hands were clenching and unclenching at his sides. He continued to talk in a low growl. "You move out of our house, you get a job, and you start seeing your old boyfriend again."

His clenched fist suddenly flew through the air, striking

the wall with a resounding blow. Simultaneously his voice emitted a barbarous yell that shattered the air.

"Stephen, no!" Why couldn't she say something more than his name? She was lost for thoughts or words. Suddenly he yanked her into his arms, his lips crushing against hers, his tongue buried deep inside her mouth. His mouth jerked away to her ear, his voice a husky, painful whisper. "I've been going crazy these last few weeks. I haven't been able to think, to work, to sleep." His arms were squeezing the breath out of her. "Jessie, why didn't you just tell me?" A cold fear stung the raw edges of her nerves.

"I don't know what you mean," she stated, painfully aware every second of what she had to say.

"Don't close me out, Jessica. I know. I know all about it. I talked to David Sinclair in London and . . . to Rosita."

She was silent, her face pressed into the security of his chest. So he knew. It still didn't change anything. She knew what she had to do. She couldn't be a burden to him any longer.

"Jessica. I did not marry you to get Benchcrest. You've got to believe that."

"I know that."

"You know?"

"Yes."

"Then . . . are you in love with Bill?" The words came out reluctantly as if he really did not want to know the answer.

"No," she answered emphatically. "I had a long talk with Dan today. He told me, Stephen. He told me about you and what you have done for the last—what has it been—nine years?"

"He told you!" His voice and expression reflected a sense of betrayal.

"Yes. Don't be mad at him. I'm really glad he did. It clears up some things. I'm just—just sorry that you had to do it. I know it must have been a terrible burden to you . . . and—"

"Burden?" He was holding her away from him, the light from his eyes making it difficult to see the path she had to take. "Jessica, you have never been a burden to me. I lo—"

"Stephen, please. I have so many things to say to you, I hardly know where to begin. But first I'd like for you to explain some things to me. You see, I thought my parents had lots of money." Her face looked lost and childlike, the face of a little girl who has suddenly realized that the world is not one big candy store.

"They did at one time, honey."

"What happened then?"

"Let's sit down." Stephen led her to the couch, where they sat facing each other, their hands tightly clasped together. "Your father was a great lawyer—and a hell of a good man. But he was not—he didn't have the best business sense. He made some bad investments. Quite a few, as a matter of fact." Seeing the pained expression on her face, he added, "Jessica, it could have happened to anyone."

"Did he come to you when he realized he was broke?" she asked quietly, finding it difficult to imagine her strong father in such a weak position.

"Yes. You were very young when my father died, and so I doubt if you fully realized what your family did for me. Your dad became the father I lost. He helped me through lots of growing pains, and I loved him—I really loved him. And he knew he could trust me and depend on me. So he came to me to help him with his troubles. I loaned him whatever he needed to live on. We had worked out a long-term financial agreement and I knew he would pay me back."

"Why didn't he ever tell me?"

"He wanted to, but . . . I convinced him not to." Jessica looked up sharply at Stephen, trying to imagine her father, who was so good at giving advice, taking the advice of a young man who was like a son to him.

"Maybe it was the wrong thing to do," Stephen reflected as he watched the play of emotions on Jessica's face. "But I just didn't want the image you had of your father shattered. I know how you idolized him. I also knew that you were the type of person who would sacrifice whatever it took to help your family. I wanted you to get a good education. I wanted you to have all the things that you wanted—that you deserved." He paused, and Jessica had to fight to keep back the tears. "So anyway, we worked out this arrangement and, as you now know, Dan was in on it."

"I don't really know what to say, Stephen. I don't know how I can ever thank you enough for all you've done for me. It's so—"

"No." His voice was hard and decisive. He stood up abruptly and walked over to the mantel of the fireplace. "I don't want you to thank me. I don't want that, do you understand!"

"All right," she replied weakly, confused by his sudden change of attitude.

"Don't you understand?" He was back beside her, his hands grasping her upper arms. "That's why I never wanted you to know. I didn't want you to feel you owed me anything. I didn't want you to feel that I—that I owned you." The liquid brown centers of his eyes were pulling her into them, demanding that she see inside his mind, inside his soul. "I thought that somehow you must have found out—until I talked to David and Rosita. I thought —well, you were so distant and cold—I started thinking that you had married me because you felt like you owed me something. I thought maybe you felt like it was some sort of obligation, a debt you owed me."

Her eyes widened, making her look startled. She couldn't believe what he was saying. She was the obligation, not him! Wasn't she? "Stephen? You mean—I thought— Don't you want a divorce?"

"A divorce?" His voice cracked with astonishment. "A divorce! You can't be serious."

"I thought that you married me out of a sense of obligation and I . . . well, I didn't want to be a burden to you. I mean, I owe you so much, and I thought your freedom is what you'd want more than anything." She was looking down at her hands, nervously wringing in her lap.

She watched his hands cover hers. "You've given me so much more than I deserve. If there was a debt to pay, you paid it in full seven years ago."

Her head shot up, her eyes darting painfully around the room. It was the first reference he had made to that moment seven years ago when she had lost her youth, when she had given herself, body and soul, to him forever.

"What you gave to me—" His voice cracked and could not finish the sentence.

"Is that why you married me, Stephen?" Her voice was barely above a whisper. "Out of guilt?" This thought was so new to her, so humiliating to her, that it caused tears to spring to her eyes.

His hands lifted to the sides of her face, pulling her head up so that her eyes would meet his. "I married you because I love you, Jessie. That's the *only* reason. It's true, I felt guilty as hell about what I did to you seven years ago; I've called myself every vile name in the book. I told myself I did nothing more than plunder your body. I took advantage of your vulnerability and love. I found myself pretty hard to live with for a long time."

"But why did you go away, Stephen?" The tormented cry flew from her lips. "Why didn't you come back? I waited for you. Didn't you know that I loved you?"

"I knew you idolized me and I suspected there was a chance that you loved me. But . . . at that time in my life I didn't want you to. You see"—he paused, breathing deeply—"my life had become so fragmented. So different than I had planned. I found myself involved in a world so removed from the one I grew up in . . . the one you grew up in. The crowd I was running with were lost and desperate and seeking something they didn't have. The problem is"—he laughed bitterly—"when they finally attained it they found it wasn't worth the search. I've seen some ugly things. I've lived some ugly lies. I'm not proud of it. I hated myself for what I was becoming. But I couldn't stop."

She listened intently to him, suspecting that he was revealing his own self-doubts and loneliness for the first time. "When I was in college, every girl I went out with was after me for my money. At least it seemed that way at the time. I felt vulnerable and lonely. So I decided that rather than be defeated and used by my wealth, I would be the user. If anyone was going to be defeated, it was going to be the other guy. It gave me power over a world that seemed totally out of focus to me. I felt if I ever lost

184

that power I would drown in my own vulnerability. But it's funny." His laughter did not sound the least bit funny. "What I found was that I *was* drowning—drowning in the filthy debris of superfluous, wasted lives."

"But I didn't love you for your money. I loved you for you . . . I always have." She had to make sure that he knew that she was not like all the others.

"And I have always loved you too. First like a little sister. But later, as I watched you growing into a woman, I knew I loved you on a different level. You represented to me all that was beautiful and good in life. You were my innocence, my youth, my happiness. When you gave yourself to me that afternoon, I at first thought I could never ask for more than you. But when I realized the consequence of what I had done to you . . . it was as if I had tainted your body. I wanted you forever, but I couldn't drag you down in the gutter with me. I didn't deserve you."

"But, Stephen, I didn't feel that way."

"Listen, honey. You've heard the stories about me in the papers. I don't know why it is, but people, for some reason, are obsessed with the seamier side of life. So I became a celebrity—of sorts. Some of the stories were true and some—most—were not. But I didn't want you to be touched by it. It would have killed me to see them crucify you the way they did me.

"So I thought it was best to leave you in the world where you belonged. You would remain in my memory as the symbol of my happier times. My innocence. My lifeline to sanity. God, Jessica, I never meant for it to hurt you. I really thought you would forget me. I thought you would find someone different—someone better—someone like Bill. But when I saw you again in March, I knew I couldn't let you go this time. I needed you too much."

Her mind was having trouble functioning. She was trying to absorb all of this information. Wanting to be ecstatic and happy, yet afraid to be. "Stephen—" She breathed deeply, wanting to ask this question yet not wanting to ask. "Why were you with Angela today?"

"You saw us?" She nodded, bracing herself for the answer. "I called Angela because I knew she was a friend of yours. I thought maybe she could help me. I wanted you to know how much I love you, but I was afraid you wouldn't listen to me."

"That was the *only* reason you were with her?" She desperately wanted to believe that it was true.

"The *only* reason."

She looked at him for a long moment, trying to absorb the knowledge of who Stephen Dalheurst was. She evaluated the man and knew that she loved him more than anything in the world. And for the first time she believed that he loved her as much. "I owe you apologies for so many things I've said. I've always been too quick with the tongue, but never again—"

"Jessica, it doesn't matter. It's in the past. It's all behind us now. Let's just think about the future."

"For the last seven years," she admitted, "all I've had of you were memories. I can't go on reliving them. I have to start making some new ones." She was smiling at him now, the love she had felt for so many years finally free to blaze from her eyes.

He returned her smile, and his thumb began stroking the outline of her lips. "You really are my lifeline, Jessie. I love you." His lips met hers in a firm, but tender kiss.

The pressure on her mouth increased, and she felt a gate

opening, knowing that soon she would finally be fulfilled in love. The fire in her body began to spark and burn as their kisses became more urgent. Their mouths were pressed tightly together, their tongues deliciously rough against each other. She was pulled against him, his hands were roaming over her body, frantic and demanding. She leaned back on the couch. His hands began freeing the buttons of her blouse and his mouth descended and caressed the now exposed skin.

She was vaguely aware of being carried into the bedroom. But the blazing fire in her body overpowered the awareness of her surroundings. The unsuppressed passion had a drugging effect on her.

She felt Stephen removing her clothes from her body as her own hands fumbled at the buttons on his shirt. The ache inside was consuming her, blinding her to everything but his demanding touch. Somehow, after an eternally long time, they were both undressed, their naked skin touching and clinging. Her breasts were flattened against the wall of his chest. His lips were upon hers, crushing and demanding, their tongues moving against each other in overwhelming urgency, greedily tasting every corner of each other's mouth. Her hands were gripping his hair, her fingers pulling and dragging his face harder against hers.

In one swift movement Stephen lifted her and lay her across the bed. She was hypnotized by the hunger in his eyes, the hard desire of his body. His hands and his mouth were covering her body, possessing every square inch of it. A moan wrenched from her throat at his touch, sending a shudder of desire through Stephen. His hands on her breasts were firm and caressing, his tongue on her nipples arousing sensations she did not know she possessed. His breath was shallow and ragged.

With love-drugged eyes she watched him tower over her, then descend slowly. The heat between their bodies fused them together, and she breathed in the intoxicating smell of his male body as it possessed her. Her hands clutched at the rippling muscles of his back and arms, her hips arching instinctively against his. His arm curved under the small of her back, supporting her weight and pulling her hips up into the thrust of his body on her. His other arm supported him, and his fingers tugged involuntarily at her hair as his mouth consumed hers with unabated hunger. Their bodies thrusted and undulated, driving them to the edge of desire.

At the moment of completion she heard a low moan escape his lips. She had never felt so alive, her body so dizzily surging, then exploding like a crashing wave upon the beach.

It was a long time before either of them moved. And then, softly and slowly, Stephen's hand began gliding over her body. Their initial coming together had been so explosive, so full of their own urgent needs, that they had been barely conscious of each other's wants and desires. But now his hands stroked her neck, her breasts, her stomach, and her thighs, his touch worshiping every curve and mound and hollow of her body. His smoldering eyes moved slowly over her face and hair and neck and breasts, the warm brown liquid centers adoring in their gaze.

Jessica felt the love in his touch and in his eyes, and slowly and sweetly pulled his head down to meet her soft, moist lips. The fire in her body was building again, and she felt the same need grow and harden in him.

"You said you wanted to make new memories." His voice was hypnotic and as smooth as velvet. "Is this what you had in mind?"

When his hand moved between her thighs, she gasped, and the emphatic nod of her head answered his question.

This time their lovemaking was slow and tender. They touched and tasted and delighted in the secrets of each other's bodies, and they undulated with a rhythm like that of the lake water lapping and caressing the rocks at the base of the cliff.

When the fires in both of their bodies had been doused and their thirst for each other's kisses temporarily quenched, they lay exhausted in each other's arms.

"Sleep now, Jessie." Stephen tucked the blanket around her and his hand stroked her damp hair. She quickly fell under the spell and slept.

When she woke, it was morning. Sunlight streamed through the blinds covering the bedroom window. Jessica stretched the muscles of her body, one at a time, like a cat waking from a long, restful nap. She looked around the room and noticed that it was almost bare. The closet door was open and all her clothes except for one outfit were gone. The top of the dresser was bare. She heard a clanging and clattering of pots in the kitchen. She was trying to make sense of the noise when the bedroom door opened.

Stephen stood in the doorway, sunlight adding a glow to his hair and eyes. His hands were on each side of the door frame in a stance of mock gruffness and authority.

"What are you doing?" she asked weakly, her breath taken away by the sudden desire she felt for him. She knew, in that moment, that she would always feel this way; she could never have enough of him.

"Get dressed," he commanded with false imperiousness.

"What are we doing?"

"I'll tell you when we're on our way."

The game became obvious. She realized the repeat of their conversation the day Stephen stormed into her apartment to take her to Benchcrest. She sat up in bed, tucking the blanket under her arms and staring back at him with playful defiance.

"You have a choice," he growled. "You can either dress yourself or I'll do it for you."

Smiling to herself, she threw on her only remaining outfit, a pair of freshly pressed jeans and a gauze shirt. She washed her face and brushed her teeth quickly, applying very little makeup. When she entered the living room, it, too, was bare, except for the furniture. Stephen grabbed her arm and led her forcefully to the Jaguar parked in front. The trunk and back shelf were loaded with Jessica's personal belongings. She eased into the front seat, and Stephen walked around to his side of the car. It was only after they were driving north on Lake Shore Drive that she asked the question they both knew she would ask.

"Now, do you mind if I ask where we're going?" she teased, knowing full well that his response would be "North."

There was only a second's hesitation before he responded, with an emotion-filled voice, "Home."